Rebirth

*A Widow, Single Dad, Curvy Girl,
Billionaire Romance*

Heart of Stone Jordan & Damon
Book 2

Chiquita Dennie

304 Publishing Company

 Created with Vellum

First and foremost, I want to thank my family and all my friends. My fellow writing partners in crime (you know who you are), I couldn't do this without you guys. A special thank you to my readers for continuing to show your tremendous support and share my stories.

Author Inspiration

"Never allow anyone to steal your joy. It doesn't matter how many times someone says you can't do something. Invest in yourself—even if it's just writing down what your goals and plans are. Starting small can lead to bigger things."

—Chiquita Dennie

Latest Releases from Chiquita Dennie

Pressure(A Driven World Novel)
Until Serena(HEA World Novel)
Exposed (Salvation Society Novel)
Heart of Stone, Book 4 (Jessica and Joseph)
She's All I Need
Something Gaine(Romantic Comedy)
Upcoming Releases (2023/2024):
Something Earned (Romantic Comedy)
The Carrington Cartel
Nicco-TN Seal Security Book 3
Something Borrowed(Romantic Comedy
Knox-TN Seal Security Book 4

Disclaimer

This work of fiction contains strong language and explicit sexual content and is only intended for mature readers. This story may contain unconventional situations, language, and sexual encounters that may offend some readers.I would recommend another book. This book is for mature readers (18+).

Introduction

Are you signed up for my newsletter?

Join today and find out all the latest in new releases, contests, giveaways, sneak peeks and more.
www.chiquitadennie.com

Synopsis

These two both have a second chance at love, but will they take it?

Jordan:

I'm so sick of struggling.

It's been that way ever since my husband passed away, leaving me to raise our son. I know that I can't go through that kind of heartbreak again so I'm resigned to being alone.

Then I meet Damon Adams and he has hope and interest burning inside of me. I'm determined to keep him at arm's length though.

Except he seems to have other plans...

Damon:

After my Break up, I swore off women. Well, with the exception of my daughter.

She's been my only focus for so long that now I'm starting to wonder if maybe I've been to harsh. Maybe it's time that I tried to find love again.

Too bad for me, my ex doesn't seem ready for that to happen...

When Damon meets Jordan, sparks fly but will their relationship be able to withstand drama from his ex and the blending of both of their families?

Previously in the Heart of Stone Series, Book 1: Emery & Jackson

P ulling up to the parking lot of my son's daycare center, I jumped out and headed inside to pick him up. I rushed through the doors and collided into a hard body, and two strong arms tried to steady me.

"Damn, you all right, Choc?"

"Huh?" I responded as I stared into light-brown eyes and deep dimples. I felt like I was having an orgasm from just looking at him. That's not possible.

Two fingers snapped in front of my face. I blinked out of my lust-filled trance.

"What did you call me?"

"Choc," he replied with a stunning smile.

"What does Choc mean?"

"Sorry, sweetness, but you're beautiful as milk chocolate." He glanced down at my hand and noticed I wasn't wearing a ring before continuing, "My favorite type of candy."

"Ohh... umm... well, thanks. But I need to..."

Tightening his hold on me, he pulled me in closer, and

I smelled his cologne. The same brand Devin used to wear, Tom Ford Musk 1991.

"Sorry, Choc, I can't let you go until I get your number. It must be fate that we met like this. I don't know about you, but I won't pass this chance up. Let me take you out," he suggested.

I shook my head and pulled away from him.

"I'm sorry, Mr...."

"Damon Adams."

"Mr. Adams."

"Damon, and you are?"

"Jordan Davis."

"Nice to meet you, Choc."

Smirking at his comment, I shook my head and turned to look around to make sure the teachers hadn't dismissed the students yet.

"Jordan is my name, and Mr. Adams—"

"Call me Damon, beautiful."

"Fine, Damon... I don't date, and I'm here picking up my son."

"Small world. I'm picking up my daughter. What class is he in?"

"I'm not in the habit of giving out my private business to strangers. Check with some of the teachers around here. They may be right up your alley."

I turned and walked away, praying he couldn't smell my arousal from the throbbing heat between my legs. I needed a release and standing in his arms didn't help.

"How about lunch?" he called out.

"No."

"How about dinner?"

"No."

"How about ice cream?"

"No—"

"Yeah, Mommy, ice cream!" Devin Jr. screamed excitedly, running into my legs.

"Hi, Mrs. Davis. He couldn't wait to see you and show off the picture he drew," DJ's teacher Amy Lawrence stated.

I rolled my eyes at Damon's smug look at my son's outburst for ice cream, probably hoping to guilt me into complying.

"Baby, you have to eat first." I bent down to kiss DJ on the forehead. He pouted, crossed his arms, and stomped his feet.

"Mr. Adams, Tessa should be coming out of the classroom any minute now. I didn't know you two knew each other."

"We don't," we both answered.

"That's going to change real soon though," Damon answered, smiling at me and winking.

Chapter One

Jordan

A Year Later

"How does this feel?" Damon's soft, large hands moved up and down as he worked the knots out of my shoulders. Feeling his large presence behind me brought back memories of his soft kisses, running a trail up and down my chest.

Feeling a tightness in my chest, I blocked out the thoughts, while standing off to the side, away from the crowd. "Lower, please," I told Damon as he massaged my back.

"Have you decided to go out to dinner with me yet?"

Tensing at his question, I moved away from his arms and tightened my bikini top around my neck again. I turned and headed toward the downstairs bathroom to continue getting myself back together. After our little quickie at Emery's house, I knew he wouldn't just let things go without talking about commitment. "Damon, we agreed just to keep things casual."

"Jordan, it's been almost a year, and we've gone on

playdates with our kids. I like you, and I know you like me. Why are you so afraid to take the next step?"

"I don't want to talk about it. Let's just get the kids out of the water and have dinner."

"Jordan, listen to me. I'm not trying to replace your husband." He moved in closer behind me and wrapped his arms around my waist. He leaned in closer and kissed the back of my ear as I stared into the bathroom mirror.

"Just drop it, okay?"

"For now, I will—since the kids are around—but we're finishing this conversation."

Rolling my eyes at his demanding nature, I turned away. He gripped me gently by the arm and pulled me against his chest, leaning over to kiss me on the lips.

"Mmmm..." I moaned. He ran his hands up and down my back, then to my ass. He squeezed, and I moaned into his kiss. "Damon..."

I tried to pull away, and he bit my lower lip as we tongue-wrestled for dominance.

"Shit," he murmured. "Baby, either the water from your swimsuit is seeping through your bikini bottom onto my leg, or I just made you wet from a kiss. Your pussy's calling for me to take care of her."

"Can you two try to control yourselves!" Emery yelled, from outside the bathroom door. "We have kids running around here." She held JJ on her right hip and a plate of food in her other hand.

I'd watched my best friend find love and happiness after her heartbreak, and now, she was a mom, and the wife of one of the wealthiest men in the world. She'd tried her best to stay away from Jackson Pierce, but in the end, he'd prevailed and made her his wife. Now, they were on baby number two.

I, on the other hand, was still grieving my husband and taking care of my six-year-old son. Damon Adams was a guy I had met at my son's school. His daughter was in the same grade as my son, and we'd been hanging out for a while with our kids. He wanted more, and I kept avoiding him—except for when I had an appetite for what was between his legs.

"Jordan, baby," Damon coaxed. "Let's go upstairs for a minute. We need to talk."

"Huh...?"

"I need talk to you about something."

I saw Emery shake her head at us. We decided to sneak away to the upstairs guest bedroom for a little private time.

"Take that off," Damon demanded as he pulled his shirt over his head and picked me up. I wrapped my legs around his waist, but before I could lower myself, we heard a knock at the door.

"Mommy, I need to go potty!" DJ yelled from the other side of the door.

* * *

I ran behind DJ after he finished in the bathroom. We followed the laughter to the backyard of Emery and Jackson's home. It was a sunny day in LA, and with the first days of spring upon us, Emery decided to throw a barbeque and invite a few friends over to help celebrate Jackson's purchase of a new NASCAR team. After Valentine's Day—and the mini-debacle of Angela, Granny, and me interrupting them—we were also celebrating their good news of being pregnant with baby number two.

Damon was off to the side, talking with Brent, Jackson, and Emery's grandfather. I couldn't fathom even looking at another man. DJ's father was my first and only love, and after his death, I promised to never fall in love, only to end up heartbroken again. My only goal was raising my son and being the best friend and teacher that I could.

"Well, look who decided to come out from under her new boo," Angela sassed and rolled her eyes, bumping shoulders with me.

"Angela, you're the last person to be talking about a boo," Emery groaned.

"She has a point, you know," I teased and took a french fry off her plate.

We all gazed at the children running and playing in the pool with Granny. Emery's family was like my second family, so I knew that Granny was the one who would tell the truth, whether you wanted to hear it or not. Being in her presence alone would make you not want to fuck up anything; she always knew when you did something wrong. She'd just look at you, and you'd confess all your deepest, darkest secrets. It could be anything from confessing to skipping classes during college, all the way to admitting you met your future husband from a one-night stand.

"So, when are you going to settle down with that man?" Angela asked.

"What man?" I questioned.

Feeling someone's eyes on me, I looked across the backyard and caught Damon staring right at me. Emery's cousin Alicia was trying her best to sink her nails into him. We'd known Alicia since our early college years, and she was still the same girl, looking to score a rich guy. Damon was a single father, working as a sports agent with his own company. He didn't have billionaire status like Jackson Pierce, but he was well-off, and Alicia would love to get her chance to marry him.

"If you stare any longer, he's going to come over and wipe that frown off your face," Angela joked.

"I'm not frowning."

"Would that frown have something to do with my cousin rubbing her hand up and down your boyfriend's chest?" Emery asked.

"I don't have a boyfriend. Anyway, why aren't we talking about Angela and her problems?" I whispered and leaned closer to avoid anyone overhearing our conversation.

"Ooh, see the deflection, Emery? I told you she would avoid this conversation," Angela said.

"What conversation?" Alicia questioned.

This was supposed to be a family barbeque with just immediate family. Somehow, Alicia had roped Granny into letting her stay, after popping over out of the blue. She'd been in town for the past week, staying at Granny's house, and we'd all questioned Granny about Alicia's living arrangements and whether she had a job. So far, Granny had no answers. Emery was giving her a few more days before she investigated further. I just wanted her away from our group because whenever she was around, drama seemed to find us.

"Nothing." I sneered and rolled my eyes. It was no secret we didn't get along, and hadn't since we were in college, and she'd dated not only my brother, but also Emery's ex-fiancé. Plus, she'd gone out with Devin in college a few times and tried to break us up. The woman was a leech, and I refused to let her get under my skin again.

"Alicia, why are you being so nosy?" Emery asked. "Go help Granny with the kids."

"Emery, you've never taken my side with these two bitches..." Alicia spat angrily and jumped back when Angela tried to reach over Emery and attack her.

"Angela, really? In front of the kids?" Emery said.

"Alicia, we're having a private conversation," Angela sarcastically replied. "You weren't invited, so I suggest you head back to the hotel—or down to the clinic for your annual shot."

"Emery, I was here first," Alicia spat out. "As your cousin, you're supposed to side with me." She folded her arms across her chest and narrowed her eyes at Angela and me.

Emery waved her away, and Alicia stomped off, as Damon approached us with his daughter Tessa in his arms, asleep after running around all afternoon.

"Damon, thanks again for coming," Emery said. "I know JJ and DJ enjoyed hanging with Tessa."

"Anytime I can have her around other kids, it gives me a break, and I know she gets tired of being around her old man all day," Damon joked.

Angela and Emery giggled and pushed me forward as they walked off to give us some alone time.

I know this is a setup, I thought. "I think you have a new admirer," I said and pointed at Alicia, who was sneering at me.

Damon turned to look over his shoulder, capturing Alicia's fake smile, then moving in front of my line of sight, blocking Alicia entirely. Damon bent down, wrapped his free arm around my waist, and kissed my forehead. I closed my eyes and gripped his shirt as butter-flies rushed into my stomach.

"What did I tell you about that little jealousy stirring in your eyes?" Damon questioned.

"I don't remember," I mumbled under my breath.

Tessa stirred in his arms, and he rubbed her back slowly. Her eyes opened slowly, and she smiled at me, reaching out for me to grab her. "Jordan, I missed you," Tessa said.

I smiled and took her out of his arms, then followed him out of the house and to his car. "I missed you, too, but I didn't want to disturb your playtime with DJ and JJ. Maybe we can set up a girls' day later in the week?" I replied and kissed her cheeks as she clapped for joy with her tiny fingers.

"Daddy, did you hear that? Jordan and I are having a girls' day!" Tessa shouted as we approached his vehicle. I put her on the ground as he opened the backseat to help her into the car.

"That's great, Tessa. Let me help you into your car seat, so we can go, and you can call your mother before bedtime," Damon said.

The second biggest headache of our so-called "friend-ship" was his ex-girlfriend and the mother of his child. At one point, they were engaged, and she decided to cheat on him because she claimed he never spent enough time with her. Over the course of the relationship, he gave her a second chance, and he found out she was still seeing the guy behind his back. Since Damon was a high-profile sports agent, it was in the news and gossip blogs. After a while, he ended things for good, and we happened to bump into each other because our kids went to the same school. I later found out he was also friends with Brent.

After closing the backdoor and leaning against it, he pulled me into his arms and kissed me softly on the lips. "When do I get my one-on-one time, Jordan?" Damon asked, running a hand up and down my back. His eyes roamed over my figure and squeezed my ass gently. His eyes flashed a gentle but firm warning.

My hands moved upward to his broad chest. I enjoyed the gentle sparring as much as he did. I chose my words carefully as his nearness kindled a fire within me. "How about I cook dinner, and we catch up on each other's lives? I'll see if Granny can keep DJ for me."

He looked at me, and the double meaning of his gaze was obvious. I knew he could feel my heart thudding against his own. He bent, and I stood on my tiptoes to meet him halfway. His mouth covered mine hungrily, sending spirals of ecstasy through my body. His tongue explored slowly, gently reminding me of what I'd been missing.

"Ew, gross, Daddy!" Tessa shrieked in annoyance, and I pulled away abruptly, leaving traces of my red lipstick behind. I helped wipe it off his lips, then he took my hand and left a kiss on each of my palms.

"Dinner Friday—don't cancel on me, Choc," Damon said as we separated, and I stepped back as he got into the driver's side of his car and put his seatbelt on. Tessa waved from the backseat.

The first time he'd called me "Choc," I was confused and offended—until he stated that I was as beautiful as milk chocolate.

Damon winked and bit his bottom lip, and I shook my head, turning to walk off as he drove off, reminding myself to schedule a waxing appointment before our upcoming date.

Chapter Two

Jordan

I stepped back inside Emery's house and walked into the kitchen as Emery, Angela, and Granny were cleaning up. The men started to clean the backyard and put the fire out in the grill.

"Did you set up a dick date?" Angela asked.

Granny tossed a towel at Angela as Emery laughed at her.

"The last thing you should be talking about is dick," Emery said, "until you can get a handle on your own dick —by the name of Brent Townsend."

"Granny, you let them talk like this in front of you?" Alicia asked, walking in from the backyard.

"Alicia, stay out of grown folks' business," Angela chastised.

Emery and I giggled as Brent and Jackson walked inside with the kids.

"Did you have fun, DJ?" Emery asked as Jackson walked over and kissed Emery on the lips, then rubbed her small, pregnant pouch. He kissed her once again on the tip of her nose.

"I sure did, Auntie. Can I spend the night tonight?" DJ asked, looking between Emery and me. I shook my head, and he stomped off, disappointed.

"He can stay tonight, Jordan. I can take him to school tomorrow with JJ," Jackson informed me and hugged Emery from behind.

"I appreciate that, Jackson, but that little boy is going home and straight to bed," I answered.

"This is boring," Alicia declared. "Brent, how about we go out tonight? You're here alone; I'm single. Let the old, married people stay home." She walked up to Brent and leaned against him, lightly gripping his arm. He looked down at her and then around the room, focusing on Angela's nonchalant reaction.

"Excuse me, Alicia?" Granny spat out. "Who are you calling 'old,' Miss Thang? I could run circles around you on the dance floor; ask your grandfather." She danced with her hands on her hips as we all smirked.

"Yeah, Brent," Angela fumed. "Take Alicia out tonight, since your girlfriend wasn't feeling good. She's used to being the side-chick and running after our sloppy seconds." She went after Alicia, but Alicia hid behind Brent, smirking.

"Why are you getting all mad, Angela?" Alicia insti-gated. "If I'm not mistaken, Brent is free to date since he broke up with his fiancée."

"Alicia, shut up," Brent said. "Besides, Angela could care less about what I have. We're not together."

The entire room went silent.

"So, that being said, the last thing I need to do is fight over an ex-boyfriend," Angela said. "I'm too fly for that."

"You're so right," Granny agreed. "All my girls are fly. I raised nothing but queens. Alicia, stop instigating and come on. Your grandfather is waiting in the car, and I need to get back home, so I can turn up for him tonight." Granny hugged and kissed everyone in the kitchen, then picked up her purse.

"Don't hurt him too much, Granny," Angela said. Emery and I laughed.

"Girl, where you think Emery came from?" Granny joked. "Her momma was a product of my turning up. Now, look at Emery—can't keep her legs closed long enough. Jackson is addicted to that Stone loving."

"Okay, Granny, leave my baby alone," Jackson responded and buried his face against her neck.

"On that note, I'm leaving," I announced. "Angela, do you need a ride home?"

"I'm waiting for my date to pick me up," Angela replied.

A few months back, on Valentine's Day, Angela confessed she could possibly be pregnant. Of course, we didn't believe her because she'd always been the girl who doubled up on protection and getting her shots. I guess she'd slipped up because she'd made Emery and me promise to not tell anyone—including Granny. The problem was the father could have been either Brent or another guy she was seeing along the same time. She'd always been the non-committal type out of the group, and she'd strung Brent along for the longest time—until he called it quits a few months back and started dating his old girlfriend Lauren.

* * *

I cleared my throat and shook my head, clearing the thoughts of Angela becoming a mom. I prayed she would tell Brent sooner rather than later because this would only hurt the baby in the long run. Emery and I had both told her we'd stick by her throughout the process, but she'd been somewhat in denial—even though she'd cut down on her late-night clubbing. Her dating life hadn't slowed down, and I was afraid to know whether she'd told the other possible father before telling Brent.

Granny kissed DJ goodbye, and we followed. Brent, Angela, Alicia, and I went our separate ways.

When we arrived home, DJ was knocked out in the backseat. My baby boy was growing up fast and looked exactly like his father Devin Garcia. We still lived in the house that Devin and I had picked out years ago, before DJ was born. Back when I was fresh out of college, he'd started as a junior lawyer at his father's law firm. Our lives felt so simple back then—until that one night, when everything changed in the blink of an eye. Devin was killed by a drunk driver, and to this day, it still felt so fresh. If I could have gone back and forced Devin to stay home that night, we'd have been a family again.

DJ remembered bits and pieces of his dad, but not much, and after turning six recently, he asked a lot of questions. I tried my best to answer them or let him talk with his grandparents—which reminded me... I needed to contact them, so DJ could visit soon. Normally, he stayed over once a month to visit his cousins and family on his dad's side, but lately, we'd been so busy. Plus, we were also dealing with my family drama: my brother and Emery breaking up, Emery hiding her lupus diagnosis from the family, and my meeting Damon.

"Hey, DJ. Wake up, baby," I said.

"Mom, I'm not a baby." DJ yawned and stretched as I opened the backseat door and unbuckled his seatbelt.

"Then, what are you? Because I recall you jumping in the bed with me a few nights ago, after you wanted to watch a scary movie—which I told you would give you nightmares, but you stated with your little chest poked out that you're a big boy, like your uncles Anthony, Brent, and Jackson," I answered as he shrugged and grabbed his backpack off the floor. I shut the car door and passed him the keys to open the front door.

"Mom, we both know I'm the man of the house," DJ said. "I had to protect you from the scary monsters." He pushed the door open and ran into the house.

I shook my head and took the keys out of the door, dropping them on the side table and kicking off my shoes. "Hey, no running, Mr. Man-of-the-House. I'll let you keep telling that lie for now. Take your stuff upstairs and grab your pajamas for bed. I'll be up in a second to run your bathwater," I said. I watched as he went upstairs, and then I plopped on the couch and kicked my feet up on the coffee table.

My phone buzzed. *What now?* I thought and removed my vibrating phone from my pocket. I saw Damon's name across the screen.

Damon: You home?

Me: Yep.

Damon: How's Little Man doing?

I smiled, thinking of how much Damon had stepped up to the plate and taken DJ under his wing—even after I explained that he didn't need to, because DJ had so many father figures in his family, along with Brent and Jackson. Many times, Damon explained that DJ reminded him of himself when he was younger, and that he'd wished his own father was around when he was growing up.

Me: Driving me crazy. Come and get him.

Damon: See, you should have stayed with me tonight,

and he could have hung out with Tessa.

Me: Nice try, but the last thing I would do is get sleep at your place ;)

Damon: I got something that would put you to sleep ;)

"Mom, I'm ready!" DJ yelled.

"Okay, here I come," I answered and stood, making sure to lock the front door.

Me: I don't doubt that but let me call you later.

I'm about to give DJ a bath.

Damon: How about FaceTime?

Me: I'll think about it.

Damon: I need to see your face, Choc.

Only way I can sleep at night.

Me: You're laying it on thick, sir.

Damon: One of many ways.

Me: Bye, boy.

I closed out of my messages and put my phone in my back pocket, then helped DJ take a bath.

He splashed in the water and played with his toys, rather than getting clean.

"Mommy, do you like Tessa's father?" he asked.

"Where did that question come from?" I asked, placing shampoo in his hair.

"I like him, and he likes hanging out with me and the girls," DJ answered, pushing his toy truck up the side of the tub.

"What if I told you Damon and I are dating?" I said.

DJ shrugged in thought and moved closer to me with

his other toy truck. I grabbed it out of his hands and passed him a towel.

"If he makes you happy, Mommy, I'm cool with it," DJ said.

"Cool with it, huh?"

"Yep. I'll still be the man of the house, though," DJ boasted, posing with a large smile.

"That's right, baby."

The next day, I fought to get DJ to wake up and eat breakfast, and after I dropped him off at his classroom, I tried calling Damon, but he didn't answer. My attitude was on another level. Out of the three of us, with Emery, Angela, I'd always been the quiet one, but ever since Damon came into my life, he'd given me a newfound voice. My level of not dealing with bullshit from people had boiled to the highest degree—which helped, especially now that I was teaching middle-school students.

I set a reminder to schedule a lunch date with Emery and Angela sometime this week. Our lives had been so busy, our usual brunch dates had slowed down.

I walked back to the car, responding to a group text message Angela had sent, cursing Emery out about Alicia trying to flirt with Brent yesterday.

"Excuse you; watch where you're going," Bridget snapped. She was holding hands with Tessa. Funny, how she was acting like we'd never met before. On many occasions, during teacher's night, Damon had arrived with Bridget and Tessa.

"Hi, Jordan," Tessa greeted me. "Is DJ here today?"

She leaned over to give me a hug, and Bridget yanked her back.

"We don't talk to strangers, Tessa," Bridget said.

"But Momma, that's Jordan, DJ's mom. You remember," Tessa explained.

"Nope, don't remember," Bridget replied and pulled Tessa toward the door. They went inside, leaving me standing out front.

I wanted to call Damon, but I refused to get him involved in her pettiness.

* * *

Forty minutes later, I arrived at Lester Elementary School and parked, then grabbed my bag and headed to my office. My first class was homeroom, so I had time to catch up on some last-minute work.

I walked into my office and closed the door, then turned the lights on and jumped in surprise. Damon was sitting in my chair with his feet on top of my desk. Breakfast was laid out, with a vase of red roses sitting on the edge of the desk.

"How did you get in here?" I questioned, placing my bag on the desk. I moved closer to look at the tray of fruit, muffins, and fresh coffee.

"Lock the door, Choc?" Damon seductively asked and removed his feet from the desk. His legs were long and powerful.

Feeling a shiver run up my spine, I walked over and locked the door. He motioned for me to come closer, and I moved in to touch the flowers. He pulled me to sit in his lap.

"Who let you in here?" I asked.

"The real question is: Why didn't you call me back last night?" he said, his breath tickling against my ear. He pushed a piece of my hair behind my ear and leaned in to kiss the side of my chin, then nuzzled close to my neck. His minty breath and lingering soft kisses fanned against my skin. Every muscle in my body tensed with breathless anticipation.

Chapter Three

Jordan

"Y*ou* try dealing with a rambunctious little boy," I replied. "Besides, I tried calling you, but you didn't answer."

A relieved look washed over his face. "You look beautiful today." His eyes raked boldly over me.

"Thank you. So, tell me again: How did you get all this in here without anyone noticing you?"

"I have my ways. Did you have breakfast already?" Damon asked.

I shook my head and picked up a strawberry to take a bite, then I fed the rest to Damon. The juice flowed down his chin, and I licked the side of his mouth. He took the side of my face and held it gently, pecking my lips, then slowly opening my mouth with his tongue. He devoured my lips. It was divine ecstasy when he kissed me.

"I saw Bridget at school this morning," I blurted out, and he ignored my statement, turning me around to straddle his lap.

"Okay."

"Aren't you curious why your ex-fiancée showed her ass?" I said, amused.

"Did she try to fight you?"

"No, but..."

He held up a hand for me to stop talking. "Then she's not relevant to my life—unless it's concerning Tessa. Now, what are you doing for lunch today?" Damon inquired.

"I brought my lunch today."

Damon put his arms around me and drew me in closer. I encircled my arms around his neck.

"Leave it, and I'll take you to Sybil's," he said. "You can get your favorite meal."

"My favorite meal is breakfast, so what you're saying is I'm a cheap date," I responded, trailing my fingers up and down his arm.

The class bell rang, and I heard a knock on my door.

"My time is up," Damon said. "I'll let you get back to it. Text me; I'll pick you up for lunch." A smile crinkled his mouth.

"Miss Davis! Miss Davis!" my morning class yelled outside the classroom door.

I followed Damon, and he opened the door. The kids walked in, joking and laughing.

"Miss Davis, is that your boyfriend?" Jessica asked, walking to her seat and grabbing the attention of the classroom.

"Ooh!" the entire classroom jokingly mocked.

"All right. Settle down and open your books. I'll be right back." I followed Damon out of the classroom, shut the door, and stood on my tiptoes to kiss him goodbye.

"Lunch. My treat. Don't forget," Damon demanded.

"Thanks for breakfast."

He squeezed my waist gently and kissed my forehead. An uncontrollable smile tugged at the corner of my mouth.

* * *

Four hours later, I sat across from Damon inside Sybil's, with our usual waitress, Rhonda. She'd worked there for years and was like a second mother to the entire group. Damon was on a call with his latest client, and I picked fries from his plate.

His little surprise earlier had only caused my questions to rise in my head. *What exactly were we? Is he looking for long-term? Could I get married again?* My parents liked him—except for my brother Anthony, and that was because he was friends with Jackson.

Plenty of times, I told my brother to do right by her because she wouldn't stick around and put up with his foolishness. So, what did he do? Cheat on Emery with one of our best friends Teresa. The entire dynamic of our group seemed to fall apart once we found out what they were doing behind our backs. To this day, Granny still tried to fight Anthony and Teresa whenever we saw them around each other. Personally, I only dealt with him during family functions. Yes, he'd moved on to a new relationship and had a kid on the way, but he was still doing the same cheating routine. However, I could say he was a great uncle and didn't flaunt his bad habits around DJ.

"Sorry about that, Choc; it was a new client I'm setting up a meeting for with Jackson's club. He's fresh and new to the scene," Damon said.

"How is business going? I know you've signed a few new clients; I see it all over social media and the blogs."

"Business is good, but that's not why I asked you out for lunch. I want you to be honest with me."

"This sounds serious."

"Listen, I understand you're still grieving. And I would never try to replace Devin in your heart, or DJ's."

A dreadful lump of anticipation caught in my throat.

"I want to take you and DJ on vacation with Tessa and me," he explained. "Normally, I take her out of the country once a year, and I want you guys to join us." He clutched my hand and kissed my palm.

"Ugh, don't you think it's a little too soon? What about Bridget?" He leaned back and crossed his hands in front of him. Agitation ran across his face. "I'm not saying no, Damon," I explained. "It's just that we've only been seeing each other for a little over a year since Emery and Jackson got married."

"I know. A year, three months, ten days, and five hours, exactly. You have to stop putting up this barrier. I want you, and I know you want me, too, but you're allowing your grief to stop your happiness," Damon said as Rhonda walked over to fill up our drinks.

"We can talk about this later," I said. "I need to get back to work."

Memories of Devin burned into my mind. I stood to leave, and Damon gripped me gently by the elbow—not too tight, just enough to stop me from leaving without saying goodbye properly.

"You can't continue to hide behind your fears, Jordan," he said. "I'll give you a little more time to get yourself together, but this isn't over." He rubbed his temples.

That was the problem between us: He was ready to be more, and I was still dealing with Devin's death.

* * *

I made it home on time for once, with a vibrant DJ sitting in the backseat and watching his favorite cartoon, "Power Rangers." I opened the backseat and helped him jump out. He was always my little gentleman, carrying his bags and trying to pick up the grocery bags, as well.

"How about you take the keys and open the door for me, DJ?" I suggested.

DJ smiled with his little teeth, ran up to the front door, and put the key inside. Tonight, I'd let him pick his favorite meal of lasagna and garlic bread with ice cream floats for dessert.

We walked inside, and I closed the door, placing the house keys on the side table. The house still smelled and looked the same as it had when Devin was still alive. I still hadn't changed the furniture or packed up any of his clothes. His favorite chair was still in the corner, near his PlayStation, where DJ loved to sit and play *Fortnite*. To me, it would have felt as though Devin had never existed if I got rid of his things.

I sighed and walked into the kitchen, dropping the bags on the counter.

DJ ran inside and climbed on top of the counter. "Mommy, can I play a game before dinner? I don't have any homework." DJ said and passed the bag of strawberries to me.

"Only for thirty minutes, and then you need to clean up your room," I replied, then leaned down and kissed his forehead. DJ would play all day if I let him, so I decided to keep him on a time limit.

He jumped off the stool and ran out of the room. I grabbed the pots and ingredients out of the fridge and made dinner. An hour later, we sat in the living room, eating dinner and laughing at the newest episode of our favorite show, "Blackish."

Chapter Four

Damon

"If you'd ever pick up the phone, I wouldn't need to keep calling you," Bridget sassed, passing Tessa's bookbag over to me with an eyebrow quizzically arched.

I started to respond, but the way my life had been going with the women in it, I declined to respond. Bridget still looked the same from our college days: long, slender legs, athletic build, pouty lips, and a short bob haircut. When she was on the varsity cheerleading squad in school, she'd had long braids. She was the dance captain, and I was the captain of the football team. We'd met in a class as study partners on a project for African American business owners of the nineteenth century.

She'd been spoiled by her parents her whole life, and I'd made it my mission to continue that path, but once I caught her in bed with one of my teammates, I broke up with her. Soon after, graduation came along, and we drifted apart and worked on building our individual careers. We hooked up once in a blue moon—until she wore me down, and I gave her another chance. She promised she'd changed and wanted a family. After not listening to my own head and letting my heart lead, we ended up with Tessa. She went on to become the top publicist to the stars, and I became a sports agent with my own company. The fast-paced lifestyle of being in the public eye captured her heart, and she was committed to not giving it up.

We wanted different things in life. Tessa needed stability and not to be uprooted—traveling every other day, in and out of hotels—and Bridget had a jealous streak, which she refused to admit to herself. All she ever did was accuse me of cheating, while I worked on building my business and brand. Early on, I worked from home, so I could be with Tessa when she was a newborn. Compromising just to not get anything in return was the last straw.

"Damon, do you hear me?" Bridget asked with her head cocked to the side and her arms across her chest.

"Bridget, cut out the childish antics. What exactly do you need?"

"Oh, I'm childish now? You weren't saying that when we hooked up a few months ago. I want to talk about our relationship."

I stared at her in confusion as a smile creased her lean cheek. Yeah, I'd slid back into her bedroom once or twice, but she made it seem as though we'd become official.

"Tessa, baby, go to your room and get started on your homework," I said.

Bridget would pull this in front of Tessa to make me look like the bad guy. I'd never let my daughter see me arguing with her mother; I felt that, with our history, I tried to give her the benefit of the doubt that she'd grow and mature after her college years. Instead, she wanted to play games, and I wasn't in the mood to give in to her—especially while I was trying to keep Jordan from running away all the time because she was afraid to fully give me her heart.

"Damon, why can't we try again?" Bridget asked, running her hand up my chest. "We've both had our little fun, and our side pieces. I'm ready to get married. Tessa wants us to be together and have more babies."

I gripped her hands and stood back, putting some distance between us. "I'm sick of you using our daughter and manipulating her with lies," I said, my shoulders slumping.

"You can't say we weren't good together," Bridget added with a defiant smile.

"Bridget, I don't have time to go down Memory Lane. What do you want?" I asked through gritted teeth.

She needed to understand that Tessa would be the only thing between us going forward because a relationship with Bridget Carlson was something I'd never get involved with again.

Tessa came running out of her room. "Daddy, can I have some juice?" she asked, her wide-eyed, innocent features becoming more animated.

Bridget took Tessa by the hand, annoyed with my answer. Letting her walk off with our daughter, I allowed them to have a few more minutes to spend together before I kicked her out.

I needed to avoid this conversation at all costs. My priority was Tessa and her happiness. Bridget had always been extremely selfish during our relationship, but as a mother, she'd made sure our child felt loved when they were together. Whenever Tessa was with her mother's side of the family, I'd FaceTime them and see her playing with cousins and grandparents. We promised we wouldn't spoil her, because Bridget's side of the family was quick to give her anything she wanted, the same way they did with Bridget. At the end of the day, Tessa understood that if she worked hard, she could do anything she wanted when she grew up.

I decided to return some phone calls while Bridget was still there and see what was happening in the office. Since opening my second branch in Los Angeles, I wanted to make sure I stayed on top of communicating between offices, watching out for the next big sports star, and signing more free agents. Since becoming friends with Jackson and signing a few NASCAR agents, the Adams Sports Agency had taken off to the next level.

Bridget represented a few of my clients, and I soon learned mixing our businesses together wasn't the best idea, but once she opened her company, she begged me to give her a start. Hollywood wasn't taking her seriously as a young woman getting into the cutthroat world of publicity. So, with apprehension, I said yes because she was the mother of my child, and I wanted her to have her own career and not wait for her parents to hand money to her, like they did in college.

After lunch with Jordan the other day, and Bridget showing up at my place today, I couldn't believe my luck with the women in my life. One of them I wanted to make my wife, and the other I couldn't get rid of—and she was determined to destroy my life with her constant cycle of baby-momma drama.

* * *

A few hours later, I felt something heavy weighing me down. "Damn, baby, suck it," I moaned and wrapped my hand around Jordan's hair, pushing her head down deeper. I tossed and turned in my sleep, feeling something moist. *Is this a dream or real?* "Fuck! Jordan."

"What?!" Bridget screamed.

My eyes popped open. It was dark in my bedroom, so I leaned over to turn on the bedside lamp. "Bridget, what the fuck?!" I shouted and pushed her away from me. I covered my lower half, looking around for my boxers.

She stood naked in front of me with an annoyed look on her face.

"Where's my daughter?" I questioned furiously, jumping out of bed to grab my robe.

"She's sleeping. What the hell is wrong with you?"

"Girl, are you on drugs or something? We haven't been intimate for weeks, and I made it perfectly clear I was involved with someone else," I explained.

Bridget frowned and tried to touch my chest.

I slapped her hand away. "Get out."

"No."

"Either you can leave on your own, or I can call the police."

"Call them, and you'll regret it, Damon."

Chapter Five

Jordan

Three Weeks Later

"All right, kids, now, let's open our books and go to Page 78. Time to learn about the Bill of Rights," I said as my penultimate class of the day sat and talked.

"Miss, you can't go in there!" Deann, the school secretary, yelled as the one and only Bridget Carlson burst into my classroom.

"Are you Jordan Davis?" she asked.

She was Damon's past, but she couldn't let him go. Funny, because she was the one who cheated, and somehow, she made it his fault. When we met through Jackson and Brent, Damon had explained a little about their relationship, including the other things she'd done, like playing on his phone and talking to the gossip blogs. Now, she was bursting into my classroom uninvited.

"I am," I spat, "and I'm working if you haven't noticed."

"Leave my husband alone, you homewrecker, or you'll lose this little job of yours."

"I—"

"Cat got your tongue, huh? Damon and I are still very much together; he just keeps it private."

"I think you need to leave," I responded and pointed to the door.

She moved in front of the class. "Kids, you should tell your parents how your slut of a teacher is sleeping with a married man. I had his—"

Not giving a fuck whether I would get suspended or not, I balled my fist and hit her in the face, cutting off what she was about to say.

"Damn!" all the kids screamed at the same time.

"You bitch!" Bridget shouted. She reached for my hair, and we tussled in front of the entire classroom.

* * *

Two hours later, I was sitting with Emery and Angela at home, with an ice pack on my face.

"So, tell me again how you got the black eye?" Emery inquired, replacing the ice pack with a frozen bag of peas.

"Ugh! This is what I was talking about. I *knew* she would try something," I replied.

"Damon's ex came to the school and called you a home wrecker and a bitch, and the school suspended you for *how* long?" Angela remarked, eating another scoop of chocolate ice cream. Funny how she wasn't even showing yet but constantly had food in her mouth.

"Yeah, Bridget Carlson, publicist to the stars—and crazy ex of Damon Adams," I replied.

"You know, I can have her taken care of, if you need me to," Angela offered.

I waved her off and took a scoop of her ice cream as my phone vibrated. I picked it up and noticed a photo of Damon in bed, naked, with a woman between his legs.

I can't believe he did this to me, I thought.

Chapter Six

Damon

"Dan, has Bridget notified you about Liam re-signing with Pierce Enterprises?" I asked my assistant.

"Nothing so far, boss. I think it's still speculation on their end, and nothing is showing up on social media."

"What about your contacts at Fox or ESPN?" I said and picked up my phone to call Jackson.

"Everyone is saying the same thing. He may say yes if the contract is guaranteed for seven years, but as you well know, with any sport, if you get hurt, the check isn't a guarantee."

I *did* know that; it was the origin of my becoming an agent and not playing basketball professionally. I'd injured myself in college and decided to try my hand at working in a different part of professional sports.

We continued talking over what our options were if Liam left, until Jackson answered the phone. "I already know what you want," he said, "and the answer is the same as it was a few days ago: Still in the early stages of negotiations."

"The kid is still young, Jackson; he has options."

"Listen, Damon, I'm not the one who's trying to force him out."

"What are you talking about?" I asked, standing.

"Someone is putting it in his head that he'll have better luck with another team and franchise brand."

I had never been so angry in my life. I had a feeling Bridget was behind this. "Is that someone Bridget?"

I felt my phone vibrate with a message from Jordan.

Jordan: I know we have dinner with your family,
so I will stick to my commitment,
but afterwards, I need time for myself.

Me: It was a mistake.

Jordan: A mistake that you allowed to happen once again.

I don't have time for the childish games.

"Jackson, let me call you back, man. I have to handle something with Jordan."

"Is she all right?"

"Yeah. I'm surprised Emery didn't tell you already." I glanced down at my phone as Jordan texted again.

Jordan: She's a constant issue in our relationship,
and obviously you still care, since you slept with her again.

"Fuck!" I shouted, and Dan stood to leave my office.

"All right, man," Jackson said. "Let me know if you need any help; I've dealt with a few relationship issues in the past myself. Don't give up on her. Emery's ex is Jordan's brother, Anthony. They used to date, and he didn't take it well when she moved on."

Me: Baby, it was only when we broke up a few months back.

She doesn't mean anything to me.

I finished talking with Jackson, and Jordan and I continued messaging back and forth. Our dinner was still scheduled with my family, and I knew Jordan wouldn't back out of it now, since my mother had insisted that she attend. She'd canceled the last two times we'd tried to all have dinner together.

The way I was feeling, I wanted to drive to Bridget's house and strangle her for causing so much drama in my life.

The day dragged on, and I called Jackson to meet me at the bar. We were there for over two hours, drinking and talking about the women in our lives. He explained the history of his and Emery's relationship before they got married. I knew they went through a hard time before they made it down the aisle, but he also told me about her hiding the pregnancy and her lupus diagnosis, and then her ex trying to break them up.

"Things will work out," Jackson said. "You just need to be patient with her. Jordan's stubborn, just like Emery. And they all take after Granny."

We both burst into laughter. I took another shot of Hennessy as the bartender closed out our tab.

Chapter Seven

Jordan

I closed out of my messages and released a long-held breath. This dinner wouldn't change my view on things. I'd learned that I had to protect my peace at all costs to avoid situations like we were in now. My parents wanted DJ to come over and hang out in the pool, so I sent him over while I ran some errands before dinner. I parked my car, removed the key, and stepped out with my purse, dialing Emery's number as I walked to the entrance of the mall.

"Hey, Jordan."

"You sound busy."

"Working as usual."

"Where are you?"

"At the mall. I needed to grab something for dinner at his parents."

"Dinner with the parents."

"Yep." I marched toward Marshalls and noticed a few sales.

"Have you talked to Angela?"

"No, what is she up to."

"Same old Angela drama."

"She'll learn one day." I held up a silver silk dress.

"Exactly. Send me a picture of your dress."

"I'm debating on if I want this silver dress or just go with what I have at home."

"Where's DJ?"

"He's hanging with my parents for a little bit before I have to pick him up."

"How is work going?"

"Work is the same as usual; I love my kids." I walked to the cashier associate and passed over two dresses that I liked.

"Miss Jordan?" I turned my head at the small voice that called my name.

"Hold on, Emery."

"Sure," Emery said.

I put the phone on mute, turned, and smiled at one of my students.

"Hi, Annette." I pinched her cheek.

"She saw you as we walked by and ran in here," Annette's mom told me.

"I told my mom that you're my favorite teacher," Annette said.

"Thank you, Annette. That means a lot because you kids are amazing." I bent down and gave her a hug.

"Come on, Annette. We need to let Miss Jordan finish shopping."

They both waved, and I finished buying my dresses. I unmuted the phone to continue talking with Emery.

"Who was that?" Emery questioned.

"One of my students."

"That's sweet."

"Thank you," I told the saleswoman and grabbed my

bag. Headed back out of the mall, I tossed my bags in the back and shut the door.

"Remember... be yourself tonight."

"I will. We'll do lunch to catch up on everything." I started the car and pulled out of the mall, listening to my favorite Toni Braxton album *Secrets*. Fifteen minutes later, I made it home and parked. My cell vibrated, and my mom told me she would drop DJ off in an hour. I unlocked the door, then replied to her text.

Me: Did he have fun?"

Mom: Yes, and he wants to live with us permanently. I chuckled at DJ and his spoiled butt when he got around my parents. I walked to the kitchen and grabbed a bottle of water from the fridge. Turning the TV on, I went to my bedroom and placed my clothes on the bed. I opened the dresser drawer to grab my panty and bra set and went to my bathroom to hop in the shower. Before I could remove my clothes, my cell vibrated again. I lifted it to see Damon's name

Damon: I promise this is forever.

I rolled my eyes and got in the shower, ignoring his text.

An hour later, I had DJ dressed and ready for dinner with my mom waving goodbye at the door.

"You look beautiful, Jordan."

"Thank you, Mom."

"He's getting so big, Jordan," Mom stated.

I glanced over at DJ. "I know. It's crazy I even have a son. You remember me asking you where babies came from, and you and Daddy sat me down and explained?"

"Yep, and you cried. I still remember you said, 'Mommy, I'll never have a baby if it's like that.' Look at you now. A proud momma bear."

I chuckled at her comment, and she caressed his cheek.

"Super proud. He looks just like his father."

"He does. How are you coping with his death?" Mom said as she held her purse and keys in her hand.

"I'm taking it one day at a time. It doesn't get any easier; I know that much."

"I've been in your shoes before, Jordan. Don't let it keep you from living, sweetheart."

"I'm having dinner with Damon's family. That shows I'm living my life, Mom. At the same time, I can't stand to be in the same room with him."

"Love is a crazy thing. Just have fun with everything.

"I promise to have fun, at least until he drives me crazy again."

"He's probably thinking the same thing about you," Mom said, hugging me with an arm around my shoulder.

She bent down, kissed DJ on the forehead, and went to her car. I waved bye as she reversed out of the driveway and left.

"Ready for dinner?" I asked DJ, and he nodded.

"Good, me too."

"Is Damon going to be there?"

"Yep. It's with his parents."

"Oh, cool."

Chapter Eight

Damon

"**M**a, did you decide where you and Pops want to vacation this year?" I questioned as I took another pork chop and scooped up more mac and cheese.

As the middle child and favorite—which I liked to throw around a lot because I was closer to our parents, in case anything ever happened—I made it a point to have dinner every Sunday with Tessa if possible, unless we went to Granny's with Jordan. Tonight, though, we'd rotated and came to my parents' home. Luthor and Rhonda Adams spoiled DJ as though he were their biological grandchild whenever we brought him over. Of course, Bridget tried her best to make sure Tessa knew she was the *real* grandchild, and once my mom heard that statement, she almost banned her from their home. Bridget begged and pleaded for forgiveness, and eventually, they allowed her back inside.

Tonight, Koby and LJ came along with their kids. Growing up as the middle child, I helped raise Koby because our parents worked two or three jobs to provide for us. LJ was more worried about women than about being at home with his family. Once he graduated high school and went off to college, he calmed down and became more responsible. For a long time, my big bro and I didn't get along because he thought I was the favorite and spoiled, and I thought he was a slacker and arrogant. Now, looking at him as a father of a ten-year-old daughter Kendal and a twelve-year-old son Elijah, he'd matured. It didn't hurt that his wife refused to take any bullshit from him. Melissa got pregnant in college, and at one point, she dropped out, but my parents helped raise my nephew, while Melissa and LJ finished school.

LJ saw the sacrifices our parents went through to help his selfish ass, so he could get through law school, and every year, he repaid them with an annual family vacation with the kids and grandkids. This year, I wanted to pay for everything, and he agreed, since his law firm was going through upgrades, and he wanted to save where he could. I offered to help get him the right people who wouldn't charge an arm and a leg, but LJ was stubborn and wanted to do things alone.

Melissa was a news anchor, and recently, she'd gotten promoted to the head co-anchor chair of the five o'clock news hour. Tonight was a double celebration of her accomplishments and our upcoming family trip. I wanted Jordan and DJ to come along, so we could be a unified, committed couple—even after the fight she'd had with my ex a few weeks ago.

"Jordan, how is everything at the school?" Mom asked. "I know teaching middle-schoolers at the prime ages of twelve and thirteen can be hard." She chuckled, and Kendal rolled her eyes, since she was going to the same school where Jordan taught. They weren't in the same class, but everyone knew Kendal's uncle was dating Jordan, so she had the added pressure of not being able to do much in school without the family finding out.

"Things at the school are going well, Mrs. Adams," Jordan responded, cutting up DJ's chicken nuggets.

DJ and Tessa always got their way when we came to my parents' house. Not only did my mom fix a four-course meal, but she also fixed the grandkids' favorite foods of chicken nuggets and fries. I remember growing up and having to eat what was given to me, but now, you couldn't tell Rhonda Adams anything about spoiling her grandkids. One time, Koby called her out on giving in to whatever Tessa and DJ wanted, and she cursed him out and said, "This is my house. You can either be quiet and agree or leave." Ever since then, we all kept our mouths closed when it came to the little children. On the other hand, Kendal and Elijah had to eat like the adults, once they got to the age of mouthing back.

"Call me Mom or Rhonda," Mom replied. "I feel old being called 'Mrs. Adams.' How are your friends and family?" She passed Pops another helping of green beans.

"Emery is doing well. She's married with another baby on the way, and Angela recently found out she's pregnant. The family is doing well. My parents told me to tell you hi, and they'll see you in church next week," Jordan answered, rubbing a hand along my thigh. I leaned over and kissed her cheek as she took a sip of her iced tea.

"When are you guys getting married, Jordan?" LJ questioned.

"Can you not run her off yet, LJ? Unlike you, we make decisions together," I responded and stared into his eyes. Under the table, I felt a small hand rub up and down my thigh to keep me calm. The last thing I needed was LJ throwing his little shots in front of our parents and Jordan.

Dinner continued, and for the rest of the night, we talked and laughed. LJ finally got the picture and laid off interrogating Jordan. He focused on other things to annoy us instead.

After we left my parents' house, I dropped Jordan off at home. Bridget texted, wanting to see Tessa before she flew out to Canada for a movie premiere with her client. At first, I debated about the timing, since we'd just had the talk about her traveling schedule, but I knew Bridget was spoiled and didn't care about anyone else's feelings but her own. I let Tessa spend the night, and Bridget agreed to drop her off at school the next day.

Chapter Nine

Jordan

"So, I had dinner with Damon's parents last night," I told Emery as the nail technician put a new coat of polish on my middle finger. DJ was in class today, so I decided to take a personal day and hang with my girls.

Emery took a sip of her orange juice right as Angela walked inside and took her shades off to join us. The salon was on the other side of the building, so it was convenient for her to hang out for lunch, catch up, and get pampered.

"How did it go?" Emery asked.

I shrugged and replaced my left hand with my right to dry under the machine. "As expected, his parents are nice and laidback. His older brother is another story."

Angela wore a black miniskirt that showed off her long, toned legs. She sat and removed the gold flip-flops she'd just bought on our last shopping spree at Nordstrom's. "Are you talking about LJ's old ass with his receding hairline?" Angela questioned.

"Yep," I replied. "He seems very stuck up. I could tell Damon was about to beat his ass if I didn't calm him down."

"I met his brother a few months back," Angela replied, "before Brent and I broke up. He's cute, but over the top with his ego."

I thanked the nail technician and gave her a tip as Emery got her nails painted. "He's something else," I replied. "I focused more on his parents, though. Can't say if Damon's the one, but I owe myself the chance to try to move on without harboring my feelings about Devin's death."

"That's true," Emery replied, waving her nails around to help dry them off.

"How are things at the office, Emery?" Angela inquired. "Now that Brent's not around so much?" She'd been trying to get information on her ex since they'd broken up and he'd moved to LA.

"Work is fine," Emery answered. "I'm still finding a balance with the kids, Jackson, and being the vice president now. I wish this little bundle of joy wasn't a surprise to me and had been planned later down the road, but we're handling it well."

"DJ wants to come over for a playdate with Tessa," I said. "I wanted to wait before they got closer; if things didn't work out with Damon, the ones who would suffer the most are the kids."

"You're putting too much pressure on yourself, Jordan," Angela said. "Go on dates and have sex with men. Why do you need to make it into an exclusive relationship?"

I appreciated my girl's advice, but we all knew I

wasn't in the realm of getting with guys, like Angela was. She could date three or four guys at a time and not catch any feelings. Somehow, I fell for Damon and couldn't turn it off.

"She's not like you, Angela," Emery said. "She needs a connection. Someone to come home to and have conversations with." She looked at Angela with folded arms and raised eyebrows.

"What are you trying to say, exactly, Emery?" Angela asked, her face scrunched into a deep frown.

Concern grew on my face as I listened to them go back and forth about my love life. At the end of the day, I had to decide what was best for me and my child. Damon was a great guy, but he came with baggage I wasn't ready for, since I knew he was still dealing with his ex.

* * *

One hour later, I pulled up to the gravesite and turned off my car. After thinking about the advice Emery and Angela had given me, I'd decided to see Devin.

Often, I would bring DJ out here, and we'd replace the flowers that sat on his grave. At first, his parents wanted to bury him near his family's plot. I talked them into burying him closer to our area, so DJ would have a place to go when he got older. Even if he got married and had kids, I wanted him to bring his family here to show them who his father was.

"You know I couldn't stay away," I said. I bent and wiped the dirt off his tombstone, then picked up the old flowers and replaced them with new ones. I sat and laid a hand on his tombstone, rubbing my fingers across his name and the engraving: *Loving Father and Husband.* "Your birthday is coming up soon. DJ is excited to see you and put a new picture down." I told him as a tear fell down my cheek.

I smiled as a strong breeze came, and the flowers on the ground moved. To me, that was a sign that Devin was watching over me and DJ. He wanted me to step up and not feel sad anymore. "I'm trying to not let this break me, but it's hard, not having you next to me at night or waking up and watching you try to cook us breakfast in the morning. I still remember the day I told you I was pregnant with DJ, and you almost passed out," I chortled, placing a piece of hair behind my ear. "I've being seeing someone, and he wants to get serious. He's great with DJ, and I like his daughter." I shook my head, as if that would bring clarity. "It worries me that I'll forget what we had, or DJ will forget you if I allow Damon to make us happy," I said.

A large lawnmower started up and cut across the area I was sitting in as I continued staring at the family photo of us on his tombstone. A vibration in my pocket pulled me out of my daze. I unlocked my phone and saw a text from Damon.

Damon: Thinking of you.

A smile warmed my lips. We hadn't talked since the dinner with his parents, and we'd both been busy in our careers. Not seeing each other made the days harder and harder.

Me: I miss you.

Damon: Call me.

I felt a drizzle of rain on my cheek. It reminded me of where I was, and that the reason was lying six feet underground. *I lost the love of my life.*

I glanced back down at my phone, closed out the messages, and looked at the time. School was almost out, and I needed to pick DJ up and get him home and fed before I could decide on the next steps in my relationship with Damon.

Chapter Ten

Damon

"What are you doing here?"

"I wanted to surprise you with lunch."

"I appreciate that, but I have a lot of work to handle before my next client comes in today."

"Ohh, are you closing some big deal?" Jordan asked. I kissed her on the lips as she stood on her tippy toes and wrapped her arms around my head.

"Something like that. Listen, it's a meeting with Bridget," I blurted out and walked around to sit in my chair and pulled her into my lap.

"Ugh, tell me again why you decided to keep her on as a publicist for your clients? From what I see, she's only worried about being the star of the show."

"Bae, let's not argue. How is work going for you?" Right as Jordan was about to speak, the door burst open with Bridget striding inside with my latest client, a new wide receiver for Los Angeles Rangers Steve Wilkins. Jordan tensed up in my arms, and I kissed the side of her cheek as she glared at Bridget.

"Ohhh, look at this little playdate. Hello, Jordan," Bridget said sarcastically and sat in the chair in front of my desk. Jordan tried to get up, and I held her down so she wouldn't get into a fistfight in front of a client.

"Bridget, cut the shit."

"What did I do? Steve, this is Damon's friend Jordan. Her son goes to the same school as our daughter." Bridget stated.

"Nice to meet you, Jordan. Damon, is this a bad time?" Steve asked.

"No! She was just leaving," Bridget shouted.

I felt bad about the whole situation at the same time I needed to get my meeting started and finish up before he started with the team. "I'll leave, Damon. I feel like an argument is going to start, and I'm not in the mood or dressed properly to beat a grown woman's ass," Jordan spat, sounding just like Angela and Granny.

"Sorry about lunch. Can I make it up to you with dinner?"

"Damon, did you forget we have dinner plans?" Bridget stated, smiling right in Jordan's face. She failed to say with our daughter, and I knew Jordan was going to blow up, thinking I was seeing her beyond co-parenting. With the last blow up, she broke up with me, and I did step out a few times with Bridget. Maybe that gave a false sense of us still being together.

"Dinner, with her. Okay, you two have fun." Jordan stated, stood, and headed to the door."

"It's not what you're thinking," I replied.

"Maybe I should step out," Steve said.

"No!" Bridget and Jordan said at the same time.

"It's very clear that you and Bridget have something

going on. Otherwise, she wouldn't be so free to speak about you two dating again," Jordan said.

"Agghh, women like you are so ridiculous," Bridget chided and blew out a breath of frustration.

"Bridget! Shut up and give me a few minutes alone with Jordan. Steve, can you step out for a second?" Steve nodded, and Bridget rolled her eyes and followed him outside.

"You obviously have a lot going on, and I'm not in the space to deal with more drama from your ex." Jordan started to walk out with her back to my chest. I gripped an arm around her waist and pulled her close. She tried to pull away, and I tightened my grip.

"Don't let her get in your head, Choc."

"Then I guess you need to decide where you want to be. I can't take any more heartbreak."

I placed my palm over her heart and pressed a kiss to the back of her head. "I want this," I said.

"I hope I can see that one day," Jordan said and walked out of my office, leaving me frustrated and pissed at us moving back to square one.

✳ ✳ ✳

Bridget and Steve walked back into the office, and I ran a hand down my face. I needed to clear my mind and get focused on my business. I'd figure out a way to show Jordan that Bridget was the least of my worries.

"I see you got rid of the trash," Bridget said.

"Are you always like this, Bridget?" Steve asked.

"Like what?"

"Bitchy," Steve said, and I snickered under my breath.

"Can we focus on the contract?" Bridget stated.

"That's the best thing you've said all day," I answered and picked up the documents for Steve to sign and officially have him on board as our new client.

"So that's your girlfriend?' Steve inquired, pointing at the picture of Jordan and DJ on my desk.

"Something like that."

"She's beautiful, man," Steve said.

"Thanks, hopefully she'll forgive me."

"Not if I can help it," Bridget whispered under her breath.

"What did you say?" Steve asked Bridget, passing her the document to initial as his new publicist. She was the best in the business with bringing endorsements and sponsorships to our clients, even though she could get carried away with her personal life.

"I said we should go celebrate tonight as a group."

"Are you sure? Damon, I know you had plans already."

"I'm down. Everything else can wait until tomorrow," I said as I somberly stared at Jordan's picture on my desk

Chapter Eleven

Jordan

A good thing about living in my community was how close DJ's school was. Not only to our house, but also to the school where I taught and Devin's gravesite. If I needed to drop DJ off with any family member, we had only a small commute between us.

While sitting in the pickup line and waiting to get a spot to park, I checked in on Emery and Angela. I was worried about their little disagreement at the nail shop. Angela could hold grudges for days, and I didn't want to deal with the back-and-forth drama.

The line thinned out finally, and I pulled up to the small parking space for parents, then got out of the car. I walked up to the door, right as Damon was coming out with Tessa and DJ.

Carolyn Bennet, the vice principal of the school, followed them. She was a little shorter than I, at around five foot three. She was a sweet lady who helped me out when Devin first passed away, and I had to pull DJ out of school for a few months. We never had a situation of any type of bullying or drama with his classmates, and I was appreciative of her policy to keep parents informed about the littlest things.

"Hi, Miss Davis," she greeted me. "I was just telling Mr. Adams about the school fundraiser."

Damon smiled at me, and I waved at Tessa, and then bent to give DJ a kiss on the forehead, ignoring Damon's presence. He'd come wearing his black suit, which made me think he'd still been at the office, working. Normally, he was a jeans-and-t-shirt type of guy around his family and friends. All the women at the school wanted him, and even his secretary gossiped about the amount of attention he received from the women in the office. That was one of the reasons I tried to stay away from his office unless it was necessary.

I knew avoiding Damon wouldn't work, but I needed space to get my thoughts together. DJ passed his backpack over to me as Carolyn handed me some paperwork with a large fundraiser notice on the top.

"We wanted to let all the parents know about the next fundraiser and see if anyone would like to volunteer," Carolyn stated.

"Oh, are you finally raising money to extend the library?" I asked as Damon stood off to the side and glared at me. His cologne wafted toward me, engulfing my senses. He shook his head, grabbed Tessa's hand, and walked off. Carolyn waved goodbye to him.

My intentions weren't to ignore him, but if I kept him close while knowing that another woman could potentially pull him away, I'd be doubly heartbroken. Even after the date at his parents' home, I told him I needed a break. It was just too much drama, and fighting in front of the kids was too much for me to handle. Never in my life had I fought over a man. The entire situation made me feel uncomfortable. DJ would never forgive me if I took Tessa away, so I needed to make sure we both understood that the kids could continue having a relationship.

As the tears welled up, I wiped them away, fearing that once again, I would lose my love—except this time, he was still very much alive and involved in my son's life.

Chapter Twelve

Damon

Jordan wouldn't even give me a chance to explain about the photos. I thought things were going well after dinner with my family. The moment when Bridget sucked my dick didn't make me want her back again—if anything, I just thought it was Jordan—but when I came to pick up Tessa, Jordan ignored my entire presence. Bridget was vindictive but going to someone's job and fighting was a low blow. For the past few weeks, I'd tried contacting Jordan to apologize for Bridget's behavior. The guilt was a hard lump in my throat because I'd given Bridget hope that we'd get back together one day by letting her slide back into my bed.

Brent called to hook me up with a blind date tomorrow, and at first, I was going to cancel it, but after this debacle, I figured I might as well see what else was out there.

"Daddy, can we have Granny's famous lasagna tonight?" Tessa asked. "DJ told me he was going over to Pop's house after school."

"Tonight, peanut, it's just you and me," I replied. "I

have a lot of work to do, and we haven't just hung out like we used to in a while."

"Okay, can I have pizza for dinner, then?"

"Pizza? Tessa, you had pizza three nights ago. You need real food and vegetables, so you can become a strong young woman."

We both got out of the car. Tessa grabbed her backpack, and I walked with her to the door. When we walked in, she ran upstairs to change her clothes. I checked my messages, but there was nothing new besides work, and Brent coming into town for the rec center. Tessa and DJ loved being on the team, and once we figured out strategies to help empower all the kids in the neighborhood, our centers would open all over the city.

Tessa ran downstairs, right as I walked into the kitchen to start dinner. "Peanut, what do you think about me and Mom not being together?" I asked.

Tessa shrugged and pulled a chair over to the counter. I helped her climb up. She turned the water in the sink on and washed her hands as I opened the fridge to grab vegetables and steaks for dinner. "I like Jordan," she said.

I smiled at her admission. "You do? What about DJ?"

"DJ is like the brother I always wanted," Tessa said and smiled.

"Here, help me wash the lettuce, and then we'll season the steaks."

She tilted her head up and leaned over to kiss me on the cheek.

"What's that for, peanut?" I asked.

"For being the best daddy in the world. Oh, and can we have ice cream for dessert?"

"Little girl, you ain't slick."

"What'd I do?"

We both chuckled at her statement and continued making dinner. I checked my phone to see if Jordan responded to me, but nothing came through.

* * *

My fingers tightened around the remote control as I sat, drinking a beer and watching a recorded game from earlier in the day. Tessa was off to bed, and I stayed up racking my brain for a way to get Jordan to talk to me before the week was out. I knew if I went to see her, she'd have no choice; giving her space was the last thing she needed.

My phone vibrated, and I picked it up off my night-stand. Since I was with Tessa all night, I didn't want any interruptions, so I'd left it on vibrate.

Melissa was confirming our date. She'd recently split with her husband and shared custody. This was her first time getting back out in the dating field.

I told Brent I wasn't sure, but he insisted I should try it out and just have fun. Easy for him to say; he'd been out in LA, living the single life, with no kids and no drama from his exes.

Melissa: Can't wait to see you tomorrow ;)

Me: Have a good night, sexy ;)

* * *

"How are things between you and your ex?" I asked Melissa as she swallowed and placed her wine glass on the table.

She licked her lips and smiled. "James and I have a great relationship. We split custody with our son, so no problems over here. What about you and Bridget?" she said.

Despite my growing fear of Jordan being done with me, I knew I wouldn't go too far with Melissa. So, telling her about my personal life was something I'd leave out and focus on enjoying our meal and light conversation instead. "How is the courtroom treating you?" I asked. "Brent told me you made partner, correct?"

She reached over and touched my hand.

Suddenly, Angela appeared. Her date was beside her, with his arm around her waist. "Well, I see *someone* has moved on after cheating on my best friend," she said sarcastically.

"Angela."

"Damon, who is this?" Melissa hissed, squirming under Angela's narrowed gaze.

"This is Angela," I replied. "A friend of a friend."

Angela rolled her eyes. "A friend, huh? I guess Jordan was right about you after all. Come on, Jeremy. Let's go before I lose my appetite," she remarked and walked off.

The waitress came over and filled our glasses with more wine, and we decided to place our orders.

"Sorry about that," I said. "Angela can be a little over-dramatic at times."

"Are we ready to order?" the waitress asked.

"Yes, can I have the butternut squash and salmon with rice?" Melissa said.

Out the corner of my eye, I could see Angela glaring at our table. It was just a matter of time before Jordan found out.

"For you, sir?" the waitress questioned.

"Can I get the lemon baked chicken and Spanish

rice?" I told her and passed our menus to her. She walked away to Angela's table.

"Should I make the best of the night and enjoy you for now?" Melissa curiously wondered. "From what I'm seeing, your friend is ready to spill the beans to your ex."

"Melissa, look—"

She held up a hand to stop me from speaking. "Is she the reason you've been distracted all night? Don't lie; I can see it in your eyes," Melissa said.

"Is it that obvious?"

"Yes. Normally, I wouldn't have to do so much flirting to get a guy's attention. Seeing as how you're in the doghouse, tell me about your girlfriend, and maybe I can help."

The rest of the dinner went well, with us laughing and joking. I walked her to her car and waited for her to leave.

Chapter Thirteen

Jordan

"Jordan, you need to get over to his office and kick his ass," Angela stated.

As soon as Friday rolled around, and Angela and Emery finished at work, we all met at Emery's place to eat and talk. DJ was playing with JJ in the playroom. Jackson was still at work.

"Damon is a grown man," I answered, "and we're not official. He is free to date." I didn't say anything more—although I was already thinking of ways to smack him, and I knew Angela could get riled up in a minute and start shooting.

Emery settled on the floor as Angela paced back and forth, waving her hand around, cursing.

"Okay, is she mad about Damon, or something else?" Emery muttered.

"Your guess is as good as mine," I replied. "Angela, calm down before you upset yourself and the baby."

Angela grinned and clapped her hands together with a devious smile on her face.

Right as she was about to speak, my phone rang. "I

bet that's Damon," I said. I shifted my weight from one foot to the other, debating whether I should answer his call.

"He's just going to keep calling—or probably show up at your house," Emery said.

"What did you do when you and Jackson broke up, after you lied about being sick?" I asked.

Emery sighed and reached up, so she could get off the floor. Angela and I helped her up, and she sat on the recliner in the corner. "He ignored my calls and messages," she replied. "Eventually, I left, and Brent told him about JJ. Listen, Jordan, at the end of the day, it's your relationship. We can only give advice."

"Huh! Jordan, don't listen to her," Angela interrupted. "We can always show up at his work and take care of your little problem—Bridget."

"Angela, is violence always the answer to your problems?" Emery asked.

"Duh! Who do you think taught me?" she replied.

"Granny!" we all shouted at the same time, right as Angela's doorbell rang.

"Okay, that's creepy if it's Damon at the door," Angela said.

"Open the door and find out—and keep the gun in your purse, please," I answered.

"Child, what took you so long to open the door?" Granny spat, walking inside with her best church outfit on. She was coming from the weekly meeting.

"Hey, Granny!" we all yelled.

"I'm old, not deaf," she replied. "Calm down with the yelling."

"Granny, you're not old," I said as I helped remove her jacket and place her purse on the coatrack.

"Don't lie to her; she's old as dirt." Angela chuckled, covering her mouth.

"That's why your little ass can't keep a man now," Granny replied.

I choked on laughter.

"I really don't like you," Angela said.

"Thank you," Granny replied. "I don't need you to like me, because the Lord loves me. Now, have you figured out your baby daddy yet?" She stood and headed to the playroom to find JJ.

"Can we focus on Jordan's problems right now?" Angela bit her lip and rolled her eyes in annoyance.

"Roll them eyes again and watch they get stuck," Granny joked, walking away from Angela's tantrum.

"Remind me again why I love her, because she tries my patience every minute," Angela whispered.

"You ain't got no choice!" Granny shouted from the backroom.

We all looked at each other, shocked that she overheard.

Chapter Fourteen

Damon

Jordan avoided my calls and texts. She was playing games, and I was done with this back-and-forth shit. Bridget hadn't made any waves lately, after our last fight. So, I guessed she was laying low—or maybe dating someone new. I didn't care.

As I sat at my desk, going through paperwork, I reminisced about one of my many nights spent with Jordan screaming my name.

We had the house to ourselves; the kids were staying at Angela's house for the weekend.

I slid her skirt up over her thick thighs and hips, and my finger grazed over her sweet mound.

"Damon," she whispered.

I reached up and cupped her left breast, then squeezed and smiled as its heaviness filled my hand. Her breath hitched, and she pulled me up to kiss her lips.

"Don't move," I told her, then pecked her on the lips. My hands ran up and down her arms, then to her navel, and finally, her sex. My fingers slid inside and touched her folds, then I pulled them out again as she arched her back.

Her eyes narrowed at me as I pushed deeper. My erection was fighting to get loose. I was determined to please her.

"Please," she moaned, as she clenched the pillow and buried her face in it to cover her screams.

"Mr. Adams! Mr. Adams!" Dan shouted and waved a hand in front of my face.

"Huh?"

"Where did you go just now?" Dan asked.

"Uh, work. Did you get the new contracts sent over from Jackson?" I questioned, changing the subject.

"Yes, sir. He sent them over for three new athletes you may be interested in bringing into the fold."

"Thanks. Can you order lunch and get Jordan on the phone for me?"

"I thought you and Jordan broke up?"

"Who told you that?" I asked.

"It was all over social media, and Bridget..."

"Keep that name out of this office—and don't worry about calling Jordan. Hold all my calls for the next two hours, while I read through these contracts."

"Are you sure you're all right, boss?" Dan asked.

"I will be."

Chapter Fifteen

Jordan

It was a Saturday afternoon, and one of the things Damon, Brent, and Jackson were involved in was volunteering at the local recreation center near the school DJ, Tessa, and JJ attended. When Emery approached me about signing DJ up, since JJ had started playing flag football, I wasn't a big fan of my baby getting hurt. After talking with my parents and Damon—and of course, Granny throwing in her two cents—I was more easily persuaded. I needed to let DJ experience different things and not hover over him so much. Life was still a rollercoaster ride for me, and being a widow never left my mind. DJ's smile brightened my day from morning to night and giving him a moment away from his smothering mother to run around with other kids and take his mind off not having his dad around helped ease the burden. Now, I was one of those sports moms, wearing a t-shirt with her child's name on the back. Each parent had to bring something; most of the funds for the team came from local businesses, and having Jackson, Brent, and

Damon behind the recreation center brought in major sponsors.

"Run, DJ, run!" Angela shouted, clapping and whistling. "Smack that little boy! Don't let him get a goal!" She was being her normal, overdramatic self, screaming and intimidating the other kids and parents. She'd asked if she could tag along, since JJ played for the same team.

We all put on team shirts and sat under the large tent to shield ourselves from the sun. Granny, Pops, Emery, Jackson, Damon, and I sat on the sidelines with a cooler and chairs, watching them play the second game of the season. The team colors were yellow and blue. My baby was so cute, trying to leap and block any soccer balls coming his way.

"Angela, stop yelling for him to hit the other kids," Granny said. "You'll have the parents wanting to ban DJ from playing." She shook her head and wagged a finger.

We normally only saw Granny come out for church, or her date nights with Pops. JJ and DJ had begged her to come today, since she'd missed the first game they'd played last week. Her first response was that she didn't like seeing the babies get hurt—which was my initial issue. Then she said it was too hot, and at her age, getting out in the sun and sweating her hair out wasn't something she wanted to do on a Saturday, when she could be laid up under the air with her man.

"Granny, we both know ain't nobody going to do nothing to me,"

Angela said. "Besides, everyone knows DJ is the best player on this raggedy team." She snorted and jumped up to walk closer to the field.

"I see this will be a long pregnancy; her attitude has only gotten worse," I said.

Damon came over, wearing a pair of basketball shorts and a white t-shirt with "Dream Big Recreation Center" on the front. Brent was by his side. Damon leaned down and kissed me on the cheek. "How's everybody doing today?" he asked, walking over to hug and kiss Granny on the cheek, then shake hands with Pops and Jackson.

Emery waved, and Jackson stood to shake hands with Brent and Damon. It was rare for Brent to come out on a Saturday, unless they'd just come from playing basketball. Since he'd opened another office in Los Angeles and had Emery running the office here, we hadn't seen him lately. After Brent broke up with his ex-fiancée, we all thought he'd get back together with Angela. I guessed he was focused on his company.

"Long time, no see, Mr. Townsend," I stated with my hand over my eyes, blocking out the sun and looking up at Brent as he stood next to Damon, who was still kissing and hugging Emery and Granny.

"What's up, Jordan?" Brent questioned. "I know it's been a few weeks since we've talked. How's the little man doing?"

I scanned the field, looking for DJ again to make sure he was doing well. I saw Tessa cross over and kick the ball into the goal, and I cheered. That was another reason I was able to get onboard with the center; the team allowed girls and boys to play together. Tessa's two pigtails were jumping around her face. I'd made them for her last night, since she and Damon had dinner with us at my house.

She ran over and hugged her dad and then me. That little girl held a special place in my heart. It felt as though I'd given birth to her.

"Nothing much, Brent," I said. "Working, raising this little boy, and dealing with your crazy friend." I rolled my eyes, thinking back over the last few weeks with Damon.

Brent chuckled at my expression, and Damon shrugged. He released Tessa and kissed her on the forehead, then came to sit in the chair next to me. His arm came around my shoulders and pulled me close. "You look fucking sexy in these little-ass shorts, Choc," he whispered in my ear, turning me on. "Are you trying to cause my dick to grow in front of all these people?" He rubbed his jawline thoughtfully, his eyes covered by the low cap on his head.

Loud cheers over the crowd pulled me away from his sexy smile and beautiful lips. The kids scored again, and everyone stood to clap and cheer. As they ran off to the benches and the referee called for a break, each coach passed water around to cool off. DJ looked up, scanning the crowd, more than likely making sure I was still there. He smiled and waved. As I returned the wave, the last person I would expect to arrive approached us—wearing the skimpiest dress, with full makeup on, and flanked by two other women.

I glanced at Damon, and disgust twisted his pretty mouth into a sneer. For my relationship with Tessa to work, I'd stayed clear of getting in the middle of what she had with Bridget, and I understood that I wasn't her mother—nor did I want to be. Bridget was one of the biggest problems in our so-called "situation" because she wouldn't let go—even though I knew I had my hang-ups, too, like keeping Damon at arm's length for fear of getting hurt again.

"What is she doing here?" Angela asked, standing near Emery and Jackson with an aggravated expression.

With her hand on her hips, and her head tilted to the side, she pointed at Bridget and her two girlfriends, who were wearing the smallest shorts, and shirts that showed off a little cleavage. I knew she hung around Hollywood types, but at least she could have told them this was a kids' game and to dress appropriately.

I shook my head and tried to get up to leave. Damon gripped my leg and stopped me from moving. He knew I wasn't in the mood for her games today. Seeing as there were kids and other parents around, I counted to three in my head, so as not to unleash my frustrations—unless she *really* acted a fool in front of my family.

"What are you doing here, Bridget?" Damon questioned, standing with his arms crossed over his chest.

Bridget went to hug Damon, and he waved her arm away. Angela snickered beside us, and Bridget looked behind him and scoffed at her reaction. If Granny gave the word, I knew Angela would beat Bridget's ass, but since we had our kids here, it wouldn't look right—especially since some of them went to the same church.

DJ plopped into my lap, and I kissed his cheek, then took the towel from my tote bag to rub the sweat off his face. I ignored the conversation between Damon and his ex.

"Ma, did you see me grab the ball?"

I nodded and kissed his forehead again. "DJ, you looked good out there. Your dad would be so proud of you, sweetie. Are you having fun?" I questioned, wanting to make sure his headspace was clear.

Devin would have been twenty-eight years old. Every year, his parents had a dinner and celebration at the house, and then we'd release balloons and let DJ blow out the candles on the cake. Normally, the day before, I would take DJ to his grave and bring flowers, then we'd sit and have a picnic together. We'd talk about the fun Devin and I had in college and when I was pregnant. It somewhat helped me cope with his passing by talking it out and being around his family.

"Yep, I'm having fun," DJ said. "Can I go home with JJ tonight, Ma? He got a new game, and I want to play." He placed his left foot on my leg, so I could help tie his shoe.

"I don't know, DJ. We usually hang together on Saturday nights for movies and popcorn. You leaving me hanging for your Aunt Emery and Uncle Jackson?" I chortled and patted his foot, so he could put it on the ground.

Brent walked over to say goodbye. I guess he couldn't stay around Angela for too long without her getting on his nerves.

"You're leaving, Uncle Brent?" DJ asked, fist bumping him.

"Yeah, li'l dude," Brent replied. "I need to get back to work and fly back out. I just flew here to see your game and stop in at the office for a few days. Next month, we can hang out when I'm back in town." He hugged me and Granny, then shook hands with Pops, Damon, and Jackson, avoiding Angela as always.

Our attention was brought back to Damon and Bridget, who were loudly arguing as she tried to get around him to fight Angela. Bridget raised her dainty little nose in defiance. Angela ignored Emery's plea to come sit back down and continued arguing with Bridget instead.

Chapter Sixteen

Damon

Bridget was on another level of annoying baby momma. This was the second-biggest reason Jordan didn't want a serious relationship with me: Because Bridget didn't know how to let go.

It was partially my fault because I did slip up a few times during the past few months, sleeping with her once or twice. Jordan kept me at a distance, still grieving over the death of her husband. My goal was never to pressure her to get married again, but at least to try to see what we could become and give myself a chance. Choc wasn't only beautiful, sweet, and sexy, but she brought me peace during my chaotic life after the breakup with Bridget. She understood what it was like to raise a child and want to be committed to being the best parent that child could ask for. I loved that about her, and the relationship she had with DJ. When she ended things with me a few months back, I couldn't say I was drunk, because I knew full well what I was doing when I went to Bridget's house and slept with her. Jordan and I had an argument right after I came back from an event with Bridget. Paparazzi made it seem more than it was when we stayed in the same hotel for a business event.

Tessa was staying with my parents for the night, and I'd stopped over at Jordan's place to talk about our earlier conversation over the phone. She'd been out with her and Devin's parents, having dinner for the anniversary of his death. I'd asked if she needed me to come over. She was crying on the phone and not making sense. I tried calling Jackson and Emery, and they told me to give her some time. Not wanting to give her room to push me away further, I ended up at her home as she pulled into the driveway. DJ was asleep on her shoulder, and her eyes were bloodshot red. We didn't talk to each other, until she walked into the house and laid him down on the couch.

At that point, I couldn't get through to her, so I left and ended up in Bridget's bed. The sex wasn't even memorable, but she made it seem like it was more than it was. Since that night, Bridget had held it over my head and wanted to tell Jordan about us still sleeping together. A few times, I knew she'd set it up with gossip blogs and paparazzi to take photos of us at events, like a real couple. Even though I slept with her once or twice before Jordan and I became a committed couple, I refused to let Jordan leave me over this and put me back at square one. I'd fought too hard to get her walls to come down.

"Bitch, you need to worry about that fake wig and fake boobs," Angela spat out. "Jordan ain't got time to play with you today, but I'm more than capable to run you through the mud." She cracked her knuckles and gritted her teeth.

I stayed between them and waved for Brent to help me. He shrugged and left, not paying any attention to Angela and her craziness. Pops and Jackson walked toward us and helped keep the girls apart. Fighting at our daughter's soccer game was something I couldn't be surprised she'd try to do, since everything was all about her. No matter whether the attention was good or bad, Bridget wouldn't let an opportunity pass her by without her being in the center of it.

"Bridget, you came right during halftime, close to the end of the game, and you expect me to believe you wanted to see your daughter play?" I snapped. "Why can't you put our daughter's needs ahead of your own for once, huh?" I tightened my grip on her elbow to keep her from running behind me to fight Angela.

"Damon, you should be more worried about that little bitch and her friends," Bridget spat out, "I was minding my business, and she decided to start drama with me and my friends. Let me go, so I can talk to my daughter!" She jerked out of my hands and walked to the field. Tessa ran to her mother.

I sighed and rubbed both hands down my face, frustrated at how the day went from great to annoying. Out the corner of my eye, Jordan packed up her things, as the kids went to play the last of the game. Everyone huddled together as the referee signaled with a whistle to start back up. Pops shook his head at Angela and pointed for her to go back over near the women. Jackson led Bridget's friends over to the field and away from Angela.

"Man, you have your hands full with that one," Jackson said and patted me on the back.

"Jackson, you have no idea," I replied. "I have two women who drive me crazy. Both are pissing me off for different reasons, man. Bridget's dumb ass wants to make it seem like we're this big happy family to the outside world, and she's showing off for the cameras, like I'm her man. Then, Jordan refuses to claim me at all—unless it's just the two of us in bed."

"Shit sounds just like what I went through with Emery and my ex—besides her lying about her illness and my son. All three of them are strong women with hard heads and walls built up," Jackson said, passing me a bottle of water.

"How did you eventually get Emery to stop playing games?" I asked. Jordan would one day be my wife and have my child. Either she got onboard with that notion, or I'd kidnap her ass until she agreed.

Jackson burst out in laughter, as all the women looked over and squinted at us. "Shit, I ignored her ass," he said.

"What! For real?"

Jackson nodded and took another sip of water as we stood, talking amongst ourselves. Tessa was back in the game. I stood and watched her run up and down the field with a hard look on her face, not showing any fear. I'd practiced with her all day, making sure she knew that not only could she have fun and be confident, but she could also do anything a boy in the game could accomplish, if she worked hard and focused.

Another ball was blocked, and the other team lost by one point. All the parents clapped and cheered. Tessa ran into her mother's arms. I smiled as she let her mom go, then ran over to Jordan and hugged her. Bridget stood, watching Jordan with a lip turned up in disgust.

"Damn, she doesn't like Tessa around Jordan, does she?" Jackson pointed out Bridget's nasty attitude in front of everyone.

"One of the reasons I try to keep Tessa around DJ and Jordan more," I explained. "She brings positivity and less drama my way. Bridget will fill Tessa's head with bullshit and have me out here, looking crazy."

All the kids ran off to their parents as the coach came and talked with us about today's game. Out of the corner of my eye, Jordan helped Granny and Emery get the kids situated as Bridget walked over to Tessa. I grew tense, thinking that she was about to the say some shit to cause more problems. Whatever the exchange was, Jordan rolled her eyes as Bridget bent to kiss Tessa goodbye. She motioned toward me with a wink and a smirk on her face. The hairs on the back of my neck prickled. My chest tightened with dread about what would become of the situation with Bridget and Jordan.

* * *

Two hours later, I was home in my office working on some paperwork. I'd jumped right into the shower after I left the game, then I helped Tessa get her things together to spend the night with her mom. I needed to be alone, and Jordan wasn't taking my calls. So, I decided to get some work done instead. Investing in commercial real estate was my next goal. Brent and Jackson had spoken with me about going in with them and forming a company. Jackson wasn't necessarily doing it for the money, since he was a billionaire already, but Brent came up with the idea of forming a company specifically geared toward helping local entrepreneurs get startup capital. Once they had the business plan and finances, we'd sell properties at a lower cost to help them.

"Let me try calling again," I said to myself, dialing Jordan's number for the fifth time tonight.

"Hello!" she shouted over the loud noise.

I know damn well she's not out at some club, I thought. "Jordan! Jordan! Where are you?!" I screamed through the phone, standing and pacing back and forth in front of my desk.

"Girl, who you talking to?" Angela said in the background.

"Nobody. Damon, I'm busy," Jordan said and hung up in my ear.

Chapter Seventeen

Angela

To let off some steam from earlier today at the soccer game, Emery and I dragged Jordan out to a coed dance class. I came here on most nights when I needed to think and wanted to be around people who had the same vibe and love for dance. Jordan wore the shortest shorts I could find because I wanted her to relax and flirt a little with some of the other guys in class. Emery's pregnant ass stayed in the back and did what her stomach would only allow. A few twerks here and there, then she'd be out of breath and sitting in the chair the instructors had placed next to her. I wasn't showing yet, so I wore my normal outfit: a sports bra and sheer black tights that showcased the plump ass I got from all those squats and my flat stomach.

Brent's presence earlier today had been unexpected. I'd wanted to reach out for him and apologize again for how we ended things, but because we were both stubborn, the moment never came. I couldn't deal with seeing him and not being able to kiss and touch him the way I wanted to. I couldn't deal with having man problems along with Jordan, who was dealing with Bridget's bitch ass in front of the family. I tried my best to slap some sense into her ass, but Jackson, Pops, and Damon kept us apart.

When we got home, Jordan tried to lock herself away, but Emery and I made her come out with us to keep her mind off her troubles. Bridget was always like a little child who needed attention. Well, she found some. I would give her all the attention she needed with my foot up her ass. We all knew she went to all the major events, but when it was time for her to be a mom, no one heard from her—unless it brought some sort of media spotlight. Damon was a little famous because of his clients, but overall, he kept the media away from Tessa and Jordan.

My girl Jordan could care less about that life. She had always been a homebody; raising her son after his father's death was her number-one priority. So, I had to fight her battles—or get someone else to fight them, since I was pregnant now, and Granny wouldn't let me fight anyone.

"Look at Emery back there, huffing and puffing, Jordan," I said and waved over my shoulder at Emery, who sat with her hands on her knees. She was about six or seven months along now. Her lupus wouldn't stop her from living her life, and I was proud of my girl.

"Lord, why did you bring her pregnant butt out here?" Jordan asked. "You know, Jackson's gonna kick your ass for this."

I laughed, remembering Jackson, who'd wanted to come with us tonight to make sure Emery didn't hurt herself. He'd pleaded and tried to throw a tantrum, like a little kid. Jackson was so protective over Emery and JJ; it was hilarious. At first, he wanted to send bodyguards and a limo with us, and Emery had to fight tooth and nail to at least let us drive ourselves. Jackson was high profile, and having enemies came with the job, so I understood. Emery, on the other hand, didn't—even after two years of being married, she still wanted to keep some sort of normalcy.

"How are you feeling after today?" I questioned, raising my hands over my head as the dance instructor called out the count. Jordan and I had both taken dance in college. I was the only one who stayed with it after college as a stress reliever.

Her phone vibrated after she'd hung up on Damon a few minutes ago. He'd been calling her ever since we left the park today. "You should hear him out, J," I said. "He's not a bad guy. Bad taste in women, maybe."

"Angela, that woman is miserable," Jordan said, shaking her head in anguish, "Dealing with her for the rest of my life is something I can't get behind. He's still sleeping with her."

"So, you believe her? I mean, she could be setting you up. Like you said, she's a miserable, scorned woman. Didn't you tell us that Damon said she had cheated on him in the past?"

Her lips parted, about to answer, when her phone rang again.

I grabbed it out of her hand and turned it completely off. "Focus on yourself tonight and let him wallow alone. No, I'm not the best person to discuss relationships, since I destroyed what I had with Brent. The one thing I can say, though, Jordan, is that he really loves you—like, 'will move heaven and earth for you' type of love."

"When do you two think this little dance will be over?" Emery interrupted. "Hell, I'm tired and sleepy. I need my husband to rub my feet." She crossed her arms beneath her breasts.

Jordan and I looked at her and bent over in laughter. The two of them couldn't be away from each other for too long. She could fuss at Jackson for being overprotective, but she was just the same and wanted to be under him all day long.

"Emery, do you need your feet rubbed, or are you just horny for some dick?" I suggested, narrowing my eyebrows at her flushed face.

Emery waved us both off and walked back to grab her bag. We followed, getting our gear instead of finishing the class.

I picked up my phone, noticing a text message pop up from Robert. He worked with Jackson, and we'd met when I went with Emery to one of the games. Robert was a great distraction. I still hadn't told Brent that I was pregnant, and it was a possibility he was the father. I knew the second I brought it up, he'd call me every name in the book. I'd never apologize for how I lived my life, being sexually free, not tied to one man, and not having to answer to anyone.

Robert: Dinner tonight?

Emery's bodyguard opened the door to her Range Rover, and she hopped inside. He took her bag and placed it on the backseat. He came around and opened our door, as well. I answered Robert's text.

Me: I'm hanging with my girls tonight.
Rain check?

I hoped he understood and didn't hound me about

dinner. I wasn't in the mood to get dressed up tonight. *Having my pussy eaten could be fun, though.*

Robert: Sure, babe. Have a good night.

I replied and put my seatbelt on as Emery drove off. She dropped Jordan off at home and then me. We talked for a few more minutes about the situation with Bridget, and then I let her go home, since Jackson was blowing up her phone.

* * *

The following Monday, I opened my shop early. Lately, my clients felt neglected because I was in and out of the shop, leaving my manager Stephanie in charge. She knew how I liked things to be, and with all the friendship-and-family drama, I couldn't focus on hair. For my personal clients, I had my own suite in my salon, where they could come and go and not feel like all ears listened in on the conversations we had.

Today was only paperwork day, and then I was meeting Jordan for lunch. Emery had to go into the office early. Jordan had a free lunch period from school.

After going over the receipts and inventory orders, everything checked out, and I couldn't complain. I heard a knock on the door, then it opened before I could answer it.

"Hey, Angela," Stephanie said. "I heard from Gabby that you came in early today." She sat in front of my desk.

Instead of cursing her out for walking in without permission, I answered with a shrug, unbothered about Gabby giving out my schedule. Not up for our normal gossiping, I focused the conversation on work. "How are things around here? Numbers look good; traffic must have increased from all the social media promotions."

Stephanie offered a smile and started to answer—right when the door opened again, and Jordan walked inside.

Chapter Eighteen

Jordan

This past weekend was supposed to be a fun family gathering. The kids were supposed to have another game, and then we were supposed to go back to the house and cook a large dinner. None of that happened because Damon's baby momma once again interrupted and caused a ruckus—which we normally would have ignored, but she'd acted a plain fool in front of Emery's grandparents, who I'd claimed as my own. Plus, Damon broke up the fight before Angela could get going, but the day felt tainted because of her actions, and I needed space from him. He called me nonstop, all Saturday night and into Sunday morning. Then, he tried to show up at my house, but I was staying over at my parents' house, since DJ wanted to hang with JJ this weekend.

School was only a half-day today, so I decided to take Angela up on lunch and get my hair done. Emery couldn't make it because of work. After parking and walking inside, I waved at the few clients in the shop today, then headed to the back and knocked on Angela's office door.

When I stepped inside, she was talking with Stephanie, the salon manager.

"Did I come at a bad time?" I asked, then walked over to sit on the couch. I grabbed a bottle of water from her small fridge.

"Hey, Jordan," Stephanie greeted me. "How are things with DJ?" She'd met him many times, whenever I came to get his hair cut. Angela always took us both at the drop of hat.

"Same old DJ," I replied. "Running around, driving me crazy. How are you doing?" I took a sip of water. Lately, I'd been exhausted and thirsty a lot. Teaching was very time-consuming—on top of raising a hellraiser of a child with nonstop energy—and my appetite was nonexistent.

"Good, girl," Stephanie responded. "Living life and staying away from my cheating ex, honey."

Angela and I furrowed our eyebrows, and our mouths hung wide open. Stephanie had been married for over ten years to Leon, a local deejay in New York. To hear they'd broken up because of cheating gave me pause. No woman was safe from a man who had a wandering eye.

"Since when did you break up, Stephanie?" Angela asked, concerned. "Why am I just now hearing about this?" She stepped out from behind her desk to come closer to the edge.

"Angela, you know I'm a private person," Stephanie replied. "Bringing my problems to work wasn't something I wanted to do, with all the catty women up in here."

Angela motioned for her to continue and passed her a box of tissues.

"I caught him with some girl at a party," Stephanie explained. "He'd been going on a lot of media tours for the station, and one night, I asked if I could go to one of the parties. He told me no, and I asked why. He blamed it on being boring, and he said I wouldn't like all the attention from the media." She wiped away the tears running down her face.

"Do you know the girl?" Angela asked.

Stephanie shook her head.

Seeing her distraught and in shambles over her husband cheating with some young tramp caused my anger at Damon to stir up. "Angela, I'll take a rain check on lunch," I announced. "Stephanie, for what it's worth, he doesn't deserve you." I hugged Stephanie, then Angela, and finally pulled back to walk out.

"Are you sure?" Angela asked. "Stephanie can come with us. We could all use a little company," she joked. I was grateful for Angela being in my life. The comedian of the group, she tried her best to keep the drama to a minimum—or make us laugh by seeing it from a different angle.

"I'm so sorry, Jordan," Stephanie stated. "I didn't mean to bring up my husband. Angela told me about Devin and his passing."

I ignored her comment; I had bigger issues with Damon's ex coming to my job and announcing how they were still sleeping together. "Stephanie, don't worry about it. Do you mind if I talk with Angela alone for a minute?"

"Sure," Stephanie replied. "Angela, I'll start on the inventory orders." She walked out.

"What's going on, Jordan?" Angela asked.

"The same thing I've been dealing with. Damon's ex is getting on my nerves. I'm tired of her being so free with her mouth. You know, I don't fight, but at some point, I'm going to lay hands on her dumb ass," I spat out, then switched to the chair Stephanie had been using.

"Shit, let me get my gun. We can be out and take care of that right now," Angela stated.

"Did you forget you're pregnant?"

"I'm a good shot from a distance," Angela said, shrugging.

I sighed as I felt another migraine coming on, then chuckled. This situation reminded me of being in high school and fighting with some other girl over a boy.

"Wow, you find out your man is cheating, and you're up in here laughing," Angela mused. "Girl, that dick must *really* be good."

We both burst out laughing, until I heard my phone ringing and noticed a message from Damon.

Damon: Tessa is sick. Can you stop over, please?

Me: I'm coming.

Damon: Thanks.

Chapter Nineteen

Damon

"She just has a little fever," I said. "The doctor said to keep giving her fluids and let her rest. After a few days, the fever should break."

I hadn't planned on using my daughter's sickness to my advantage, but I wanted to clear the air with Jordan after my ex had gotten another dumb idea to try to break us up. The thought of her leaving me for good made me sick. I'd been working in the office all day and night, securing a new client. Jordan only answered if it had something to do with the kids, so I decided to make the best of the moment and get her to come over.

"Daddy, I don't feel so good," Tessa whined.

"I know, peanut. Try to get some rest. Jordan and I will be outside in the living room if you need anything."

Jordan stepped out of the room and walked over to the kitchen, and I followed her, gazing at her plump ass. It seemed to have grown bigger. She opened the fridge door and grabbed a bottle of water. I sat on the barstool as her eyes glanced around the kitchen, not looking at me.

With an effort to calm the tension in the room, I asked, "Are you hungry? I can whip up something."

Jordan frowned and headed toward the living room.

Halfway to the door, I lightly gripped her elbow. "Baby."

"No."

"Look at me." I turned her around to face me and lifted her chin. I didn't like the disappointed look in her eyes. My father had always told me to never let a woman become disappointed in you, because that showed you'd given up. I was far from giving up.

She drew in a breath. My hand was low on her back, above her butt, and I pulled her close to my chest. I ran a hand up and down her back, then leaned down to meet her halfway with a kiss. I took her hand and led her to my bedroom. I figured my best chance was to give her what she needed from me, and that was security and reassurance. She was still dealing with the death of her husband, even as she was falling in love with me and thinking that someone else had my attention.

"I just want to talk, Choc," I explained. "Get comfortable on my bed and let me take a shower."

Chapter Twenty

Jordan

"Fine." I removed my shoes and slid on top of the covers on his bed, praying I didn't completely lose my shit. This back and forth was exhausting and tiresome. For a woman over thirty years old to try to keep a man who didn't want to be kept was ridiculous. I picked up the remote and turned on the TV, pausing on the Steve Harvey Show and of course, he was talking about dating people with kids. Fifteen minutes later, Damon walked out of the shower, wearing only a towel hanging low from his waist. I couldn't get distracted from confronting him about his status with Bridget. He walked over, lifted my chin, and gazed into my eyes. He leaned over and tried to kiss me on the lips, and I turned away.

"What did I do?"

"You already know what the problem is. I don't understand why you don't deal with her," I spat and smacked his hand away, right as I jumped up to put some space between us. His nearness was too much for me not to fall into the trap of forgiving without dealing with our issues head on.

"The only person I want is you," Damon said before he walked over to the dresser and grabbed a pair of boxers and put them on, along with a t-shirt.

"It doesn't feel like that because once again, Bridget feels comfortable enough to spread the word to everybody about how you're still sleeping together."

"I can't control what other people think. The only ones who matter to me is you and Tessa. I will speak with Bridget again if that'll make you feel better."

Damon headed toward me and closed the gap between us. He secured a hand around my waist and pulled me in closer.

"I can't keep doing this with you. I care about you, Damon, but I love myself more, and my son. The back and forth can't continue otherwise—" He cut me off before I could finish and kissed me on the lips.

"Don't even let that get in your head. I'm here for the next fifty or more years."

"You can't promise that, Damon."

"Jordan, I'm not Devin, but you have your issues that constantly get in our way of building a life together that you need to figure out."

"You don't think I know that? Your little girlfriend sure gets into your head somehow, that I'm not in this with you, digging into my past. Putting my business in the media. I've tried plenty of times to let you be happy with her. You keep pursuing me."

"Listen, let's just relax and have dinner. We can talk some more, but we're not breaking up, and Bridget's the mother of my daughter. I'll always care about her in that light. Otherwise, she means nothing to me." I nodded in understanding, letting his words sink in. He pulled away and grasped my hand, and we walked downstairs to the kitchen to make dinner together.

After dinner and continuing to talk about what I needed going forward, we fell asleep together in his bed, wrapped in each other's arms.

* * *

The next morning after our dinner and long conversation, we came to an agreement of where we wanted to go as a couple. Bridget would be put on the back burner in our lives going forward. We had breakfast and fell back to sleep. A few hours later, I woke up to intense pressure down below.

"Mmm," I moaned as I felt Damon's finger rub against my clit. I felt my orgasm coming as he continued to please me.

Damon gazed deep into my eyes. He kissed from my right inner thigh, across to my left, and moved up to my belly button. Then he cupped my left breast and twirled his tongue around my nipple. His large body hovered over me as his long, thick girth poked me in the stomach. Damon was completely naked on top of me, and I opened myself wider for him without any hesitation. He knew how to get me turned on.

"Oh, Damon!" I screamed, then arched my back and tried to grip his manhood and put him inside myself.

"Baby, you ready for me?"

I nodded, knowing full well I couldn't handle his large girth. On many occasions, I tried to ride him, but often, I couldn't last long, and he always joked about me taking him fully. "Yes, please," I stuttered, stroking his manhood.

He smacked my hand away and eased his cock into my sex. We both moaned at the slow penetration. "This what you've been needing, Choc?" Damon grunted, slowly thrusting in and out.

I was speechless as he lowered himself fully over my body.

He pulled my hands over my head, then held them with one hand. He picked up my left leg and wrapped it around his waist for deeper penetration.

"Oh, fuck!" I cried.

Damon stuck his tongue in my mouth, not letting me up for air. My eyes fluttered shut, and his movements grew faster. "Are you finally done running, Choc?" he panted as he repeatedly slammed deep inside me.

I nodded. I was done running, and I knew that after this last big argument, I'd been close to losing him. The kids had a sleepover with JJ. Tessa was still under the weather, so she missed the fun, but we put her to bed early. We had the night to reconnect without interruption. I figured he was planning to make me finally decide what we would be going forward.

"I can't hear you, baby." Damon was fucking me into submission, and I had no complaints. He let me know I belonged to him, and he belonged to me.

"Ahhh, Damon!" I shouted.

He pulled out and turned me around, then helped me arch my back. He gripped my hair in his hands and tilted my head to the right, then kissed me again as he lined up his cock with my sex. "Goddamn, this feels so good,

Choc," Damon whispered under his breath. He leaned against my sweaty back and trailed kisses up to my neck and shoulder. Our thrusts became in sync as I heard the slapping of our skin and our low moans and grunts.

Usually, we'd go three or four rounds, but I was already exhausted, and I knew that after this second orgasm, I wouldn't have any more energy for the rest of the day.

* * *

Two hours later, we ordered some food from the Thai restaurant around the corner and lay in bed. I wore his t-shirt, and he was in his boxers.

"Any regrets?" Damon demanded. "Speak now or forever hold your peace." He scooped more spicy noodles onto his plate.

"DJ loves you and Tessa," I answered honestly. "I doubt I could get rid of you without hurting my son." We stared into each other's eyes.

"That little boy is something else," Damon said sincerely. "You did a good job with him, Jordan. I'd never try to replace his father; I just want to be a part of your life, if you'll allow me." He tilted my chin up and kissed me on the lips.

"What about Bridget?" I asked after we pulled away from the kiss.

"Bridget who?" Damon asked as he kissed my cheek. He walked to the bathroom and shut the door. A few seconds later, I heard the water running.

As soon as Damon came out of the bathroom, he plopped back onto the bed with his back against the headboard and pulled me up to straddle his lap. He ran his fingers over my smooth skin. I stole a quick kiss as our eyes connected, fantasizing about moving forward as an official couple.

"I keep telling you," he said. "Bridget is the least of my worries. Don't let her come between what we could have, Jordan." He pointed between us, then leaned forward.

I met him halfway as he kissed my forehead. "You're right, but I don't want Tessa to not have the opportunity to grow up and have a two-parent household. What if she comes to me one day and asks why her mom and dad aren't married?" I inquired.

His fingers stroked featherlight touches over my inner thigh. "Miss Davis, are you proposing to me?" Damon joked.

"What?! No—"

He cut off my reply with another kiss on the lips. "Baby, relax. I *do* plan on making you my wife one day. As for Tessa, she'll be fine. That little girl loves you. She knows who her mother is and understands that her mom and dad love her very much. It doesn't mean we need to be in a relationship to parent her."

I felt like a petulant teenager, mad at her boyfriend, with my arms crossed over my chest, and my lips puckered in a pout. I tried to climb off his waist.

He only tightened his hold. "You look sexy when you pout, baby."

"Whatever."

* * *

The next morning, after leaving Damon's home, I had to meet my brother to talk about my parents' upcoming wedding anniversary party. Anthony met me at my home, since the kids were still at Emery's house. I knew the last thing Jackson would allow was Emery around Anthony's conniving ass. Don't get me wrong, I love my brother, but he tried to get Emery back every time he saw her, as though she wasn't a married woman with a second baby on the way.

"What's up, Jordan?" Anthony said, walking out of my kitchen with a sandwich and a beer in his hand, like he lived there.

"Anthony, I told you to stay out of my fridge," I chastised. "You don't pay any bills here, and you always eat me out of house and home whenever you come over."

Anthony waved me off and sat on the couch, then kicked his shoes off, getting comfortable.

"Boy, if you don't act like you got some sense and put your shoes back on..." I trailed off. "Your feet smell like a cat died."

"What's with the attitude, sis? Did your little boyfriend not give you any dick? I told you, I'd hook you up with my friend. He just broke up with his baby momma."

"Are you talking about the friend who has six kids by four different women and just got off house arrest?" I questioned, glaring at my brother as he took a large bite of his ham sandwich. Annoyed, I ripped it out of his hand and jumped up to toss it in the garbage.

"Life is too short to judge, Jordan. Devin was my dude, but you need to move on—wait a minute, aren't you already dating some guy who has a baby momma, anyway?"

The last thing I would ever do with my brother was talk about my love life. I ignored his comment and sat back down, then picked up the pen and paper off the table to get the party planning underway. "Mind your business and let's focus on the party for Momma and Daddy. I already rented the hall; we just need to get the final touches for the cake and the entertainment planned, since we hired the coordinator, and she's taken care of the bigger issues."

Anthony nodded, and we got into picking the entertainment for the party from the list of bands the coordinator said she'd used over the years.

* * *

As soon as I finished the last-minute details with Anthony, I went to Granny's house, since Emery texted that she was there with the kids. Tessa was included, as well, so I tried to text Damon, but I didn't get a reply. I parked my car and stepped outside in my long-sleeved t-shirt dress and a pair of Vans I'd found in my closet that Devin had bought me a few years back.

Finally feeling content with my relationship with Damon, I'd called and talked with Devin's parents and explained that I was dating and bringing him around DJ. They'd both asked me to bring him over for dinner one day. I told them I would, and that he was a single father, as well.

As I walked inside, I could hear laughter and kids running and playing throughout the house.

"Look who decided to finally show up," Angela said.

Damon was across the room, talking with Pops and Jackson as Tessa ran around his legs and between the group with JJ. Damon turned around at Angela's comment to see who she was talking about, and our eyes connected.

"Jordan! Can I sleep at your place tonight, please?" Tessa pleaded as she sat on the couch, and I checked her temperature on her forehead with the back of my palm. She was the spitting image of her father.

Granny walked into the living room. "What is all this noise about in here?"

"Your grandkids running amok because Jordan finally arrived," Angela remarked.

I walked over, right as Damon met me halfway and pulled me into a hug, then pressed his lips to mine. He wrapped an arm around my waist and whispered in my ear, "What took you so long?"

"Sorry. I was meeting my brother about my parent's anniversary party," I replied.

We pulled apart, and he went back to the corner of the room and continued talking with Jackson and Pops. Tessa scrambled out of my arms. I let her go and relaxed on the couch with Angela and Emery, watching the latest entertainment news on Granny's new fifty-two-inch TV that Emery purchased. Her grandparents were spoiled rotten, and it didn't just come from Jackson. All of us wanted to give back in some way, and we did so with little trips, gifts, and upgrades to the house. Most of all, having the grandkids around them kept them young.

Granny sat on Pops' lap, and he wrapped an arm around her waist. They'd been married for over fifty years and still couldn't keep their hands off each other.

"Granny, are you still coming to the party for my parents?" I asked, passing the remote to DJ.

Before she could reply, there was a breaking news alert on the entertainment gossip channel. "*The latest scandal to hit Hollywood and the sports world is celebrity publicist to the stars, Bridget Carlson, and Damon Adams' love life,"* the anchor announced. *"This video and photo shows it's heating back up!"*

"What the fuck?!" Angela yelled and snatched the remote out of DJ's hand.

All eyes turned to the TV to see a shot of Bridget, walking out of a café with shades on, smiling and laughing, not caring that nude photos and a sex tape had been spread all over the news and social media.

My phone vibrated, and a message popped up.

"Emery, take the kids to the other room," Pops stated. "They don't need to see this."

"Daddy, look! That's Mommy on TV!" Tessa jumped up, screaming and clapping as a family photo of her, Bridget, and Damon flashed across the screen.

"Tessa, go in the kitchen with JJ and DJ, baby," Damon said, stroking her hair and planting a kiss on her forehead. He walked over to sit by me, and I jerked away from his hand.

"Don't touch me," I said and hopped off the couch.

"Jordan, I can explain," Damon said. "Please, let's talk about this at home."

"No need to explain," I replied. "I can't compete with that, and I'm not trying to, either. Granny, tell Tessa and JJ bye for me and send DJ out to my car." I felt like a fool for dealing with someone so high profile and not expecting this to happen. Bridget was right; he would always belong to her, and nothing I did would replace what they had in his heart.

"Jordan, you're upset," Angela said. "Maybe you should calm down before you get behind the wheel."

"I'm not about to chase after you, Jordan," Damon

said. "We promised, no more running. I'll have my lawyer look into this and get everything taken down."

DJ came out of the kitchen with his backpack and toys. I grabbed his hand. Damon reached out to stop me, and I waved him off to leave me alone. He tried to follow us, and Jackson stopped him at the door.

Chapter Twenty-One

Damon

Right after Jordan left, I asked Emery if she could watch Tessa for a few hours, while I found Bridget and got this bullshit fixed. She thought she was slick, putting out old photos and videos we made back when we were still together.

I drove down the highway toward her place. Since it was all over the news, she couldn't hide out for too long. I'd already called my lawyer and had the photos and videos taken down, but he said magazines would probably still run the story, since celebrity nudes made a large amount on the market.

I shook my head as I pulled up to her place and saw multiple paparazzi cars lined up outside. She was standing outside, giving an interview with either her stylist or makeup artist. Either way, she wouldn't be smiling for long.

As I got out of the car, a few photographers spotted me and came over, shoving cameras in my face. Out of the corner of my eye, I saw a small smirk on Bridget's face. I pushed my way through the crowd, yanked Bridget away, and slammed the door behind me.

"What do you want, Damon?" Bridget asked with a smile.

"Are you so desperate, Bridget, that you'd embarrass your family and child, all for my attention?" I asked.

She shrugged, like what I said didn't mean a thing. "Baby, you should have called before you came over. I could have cooked you something to eat. Where is Tessa?" Bridget asked.

"What part of me telling you that the only thing we have in common is our daughter don't you understand, huh?! Bridget, you're a real piece of work, and I sat here, defending you to my friends and family, thinking you've changed," I spat out and closed the space between us.

"That photo and video will blow over soon. You know how they get with the hottest story of the moment. Besides, we looked good, and TMZ wants to do an interview with us. Maybe even a reality show," Bridget said and reached for my hand.

I jerked out of her hold. "Stop with the bullshit, Bridget!" I yelled angrily and closed in on her.

Bridget jumped at the sound of my voice and stepped back to put space between us. "It's that bitch who's keeping us from being a family. Janet, Janice, whatever her name is."

"Are you so self-absorbed that you can't take personal responsibility for your own actions?"

"Tessa needs a family, the same way we had growing up. She deserves to come home to a two-parent household. I'll get the photos taken down—if you promise to come home."

"Tessa needs her mother to grow the fuck up. Leave me alone—or else."

"Those photos would look good for a custody case. I know a judge who loves keeping kids with their mothers. One phone call from me, and you can kiss your custody rights goodbye—unless you drop that little bitch, Jordan, and come back where you belong," Bridget said excitedly.

I knew about all the tricks Bridget had pulled in college to keep the other girls away: telling people we'd gotten married and that she was pregnant with twins. She'd caused me to miss a class I needed to graduate because she kept fucking with my schedule, since she worked in the campus office. She cheated but kept me on the backburner. I couldn't date other people, but she had free rein. Still, I couldn't believe that she was stooping so low as to take my daughter away because of her jealousy. Tessa was my heart and having to deal with a back-and-forth court battle was something she knew I wouldn't put our daughter through. Once she crossed me, I tended to forgive—even giving her the benefit of the doubt—but at some point, she'd realize the same Damon from college was no longer there.

"Is that supposed to scare me, Bridget?" I asked. "Take me to court; I promise I'll make that the last time you ever see Tessa again. She'd probably be better off without you."

"That bitch has your mind so twisted, you can't think straight. How do you think she'll feel about the new baby coming?" Bridget said and rubbed her stomach with a smirk.

"Whoever the father is, tell him I said good luck."

I finally realized that Bridget wasn't playing with a full deck. She had powerful friends on her side, but the last thing the courts would do was give her full custody. She barely got to have Tessa anymore after her little stunt a few months back, when she made Jordan believe I cheated. Plus, she was always calling me to pick up Tessa from school because she was off gallivanting on some trip with a client. I ran my own business, but I still made time for what was important.

I pushed my shaking hands into my pants pockets. She tried to close the space between us, and I turned away, leaving her alone to sit with her thoughts. I headed to my car. My phone vibrated in my hand, and I took it out of my pocket. My publicist was calling, and I decided to answer as I opened my car and got inside. "How bad is it?" I inquired.

"How bad is it?!" Linda angrily spat out. "Damon, you know Bridget is a ticking time bomb, and this is the third or fourth time she's caused problems that I needed to clean up."

I blew out a frustrated breath as I pulled away from Bridget's place. "It's *that* bad?" I questioned amusingly.

"You know I'm good at what I do. She tried to sell a story to Radar Online about you guys getting back together and having a baby. I put a stop to it, though. You owe me a vacation to Bermuda—plus, a shopping spree in Paris."

After I listened to Linda rake me over the coals for twenty more minutes, I pulled up to Jordan's home and parked next to her car. "Linda, I appreciate you. Tell Dan to set up your vacation, and you give the kids a kiss for me."

Chapter Twenty-Two

Jordan

I knew I was overemotional, and after talking with the girls and Granny, I took a test and found out I was pregnant. Deep down, I was excited, but at the same time, I was worried because I'd be attached to the baby's father for the next eighteen years—along with Bridget.

Damon finally walked inside after sitting in his car for the last ten minutes on the phone. He sat on the couch and wrapped his arms around me, then pulled me close and kissed my forehead. I felt his firm grip tighten, willing me not to pull away. "I swear, those photos and videos happened before we were together, Choc," Damon said and pulled me into his lap to straddle him.

A lump in my throat caused me to choke up at his words. "She's never going to let you go," I whispered and tried to move off his lap.

A frown appeared across his face. We stared into each other's eyes for the longest time. His gaze lifted, and his eyes narrowed. I held my breath for the longest time.

"Are you pregnant?" he asked.

"What?!" I shrieked and tried to move away again. Yes, I was carrying his child, but I wasn't ready to discuss it yet. I'd just barely found out myself, and I needed to double check with a doctor before making any decisions.

"You've been extra sensitive and emotional these last few weeks," he explained.

"Sensitive?!" I yelled and crossed my arms over my chest.

He chuckled deeply and richly, then leaned over to kiss my cheek and my lips. "Baby, I'm sorry, but you're looking a little fuller in the behind area—which I like, but I think we should get you checked out with a doctor. If stress causes you to miscarry because of my ex, I'll have no choice but to call my lawyer."

"Call your lawyer?" I questioned.

"Yeah, because Granny will probably try to kill me— after I kill Bridget."

"Damon," I said.

He shook his head, standing and closing the gap between us. "Will you marry me?"

"What?!"

"Whether you're pregnant or not, I was going to propose to you, and this only makes me love you more, knowing you're giving me another baby."

"We don't—"

"I know, and this is happening, Choc. We won't let Bridget come between what we're building. You love me?"

I nodded—even though deep down, I was angry, hurt, and furious at Bridget once again. I knew Damon was right; I couldn't let her rile me up.

* * *

One week later, we confirmed with a doctor that I was pregnant. DJ ran around, telling everyone at school and all our friends that he was going to be a big brother.

The entire family and all our friends came together for my parents' anniversary party. I even invited Devin's parents. Emery and Angela sat next to me as Anthony stood up to say a few words about our parents. He'd had too many drinks, so our dad pulled him offstage and told the staff to bring him some coffee. I couldn't believe he'd decided to act like an ass at our parents' event. The night had been going great—before he tried to flirt with Emery, but Jackson wasn't having that and told him that if he stepped to her one more time, he'd make him disappear. Of course, I believed him. Since the man was a billionaire, he had the means to make it happen. Amusement glinted in his dark eyes as Emery spoke with Pops and Granny on my right.

"I swear, my brother is an idiot. He reminds me so much of Bridget; they can't take rejection and continue to live in a bubble."

Damon came up behind me, pressed his chest to my back, and wrapped a hand around my waist, then kissed my shoulder. "Choc, no stressing. Tonight is about your parents' anniversary and our engagement. Your mom already is thinking about baby names," Damon muttered and kissed my ear.

My lips quirked, and I rolled my eyes. This would be a long pregnancy, between Granny, my parents, and Damon's parents. Even Emery and Angela could be over-whelming at times. "Don't remind me," I replied.

Damon turned me around to face him and lifted my chin. "Ready for forever?" he asked.

"No, but if you're next to me, I know I'll be okay," I said.

Chapter Twenty-Three

Damon

After talking with her parents and Devin's family after the engagement party, we decided to come together to his grave. Jordan needed to finally know that Devin wouldn't want her to be stuck in limbo and never love again. I wouldn't allow that—especially with my baby growing inside her. We brought DJ and Tessa with us, so Tessa would know who DJ's father was.

Bridget wasn't answering my calls when Tessa wanted to see her, so my lawyer set up an agreement through her parents as the mediator to discuss visitation. Granny was the one to help me see that Bridget wasn't ready to let me go, and she told me to keep an eye out for more trouble. I promised I would because the alternative was Granny bringing out the big guns, and I believed she would.

I didn't want to see Bridget hurt, but she needed someone to smack some sense into her. My engagement to Jordan and her pregnancy was already plastered all over the entertainment blogs and the news. Someone on

Emery's staff spilled the beans at the anniversary party. We couldn't go out without the paparazzi hounding us.

Jordan nudged me out of my thoughts and stood on her tiptoes. I bent down, meeting her halfway for a kiss. The sun was shining, and the air was crisp. I felt like a new start for our family could finally get things moving in the right direction.

"Devin," she said to his grave, "I'll always love you, and you know I'll keep your memory alive in our son, but I have to finally move on." She placed the flowers down, cleaning around his gravesite.

When she finished, she stood, and I held her hand tightly.

"You remind me of Devin," she said to me. "The way you protect me and care for me."

"I'll always protect you, Choc—even if it's from me," I said and pecked her lips.

"We should get going," she replied. "The kids are hungry, and I have too much work to catch up on after this long week."

"What are you in the mood for, DJ and Tessa?" I asked, peering around Jordan to watch DJ and Tessa help clear off the headstone.

"Can we have pizza, Daddy?" DJ asked. Without warning, he came over and hugged my legs.

I smiled and felt the weight of the world on my shoulders when DJ called me "Daddy." That little boy wasn't mine biologically, but I'd lay my life on the line for him if anyone ever tried to hurt him. I bent, picked him up, and kissed his forehead. "Pizza it is, little man. Let's go home," I said.

I grabbed Jordan's hand, and she gripped Tessa's, and we walked to the car.

* * *

The next day, I was at work, going over paperwork before my trip to Vegas with Jordan. I had a conference call with Brent and Jackson to talk about the next big rec center event.

"Okay, so, we have a few ideas for our next event," Brent said. "Maybe a tournament or a fair of some kind to bring all the schools together. I know we can get the local stations to air it and put some media contacts on the field."

"How's the LA dating life, Brent?" Jackson questioned.

Getting over Angela didn't seem to have slowed him down. Every other day, he was with a new girl, living the single life. "Man, if you weren't married to my best friend, I'd tell you to come out here," Brent joked. "The chicks are everything and more." He bit his bottom lip and rubbed his hands together.

"Dude, you were just engaged a few months back and crying over her breaking up with you." I chuckled.

Brent shrugged and waved me off. "I'm not like you two, getting married at the drop of a hat. It's not for me."

"How is Jordan feeling about the pregnancy?" Jackson asked.

Jordan was going to put in some time off from work to relax and get our house in order for the new baby. The thought of her giving birth to our baby was a dream come true for me. I gazed at the picture of Jordan, DJ, and Tessa on my desk and smiled thoughtfully.

"Look at that fool," Brent said. "Off in La-La Land, cheesing hard, thinking about Jordan."

"Yep," I admitted. "Just a matter of time before she's wearing my ring and has my last name."

Chapter Twenty-Four

Jordan

One **Month Later**

"Damon, do you take Jordan to be your wife?" the minister asked.

After the last big blow-up, we'd skipped off to Vegas and decided to get married. Damon tore all my walls down and helped me heal from Devin's passing. He'd stayed up late with me and let me talk his ear off about the relationship I had with Devin. I felt like I was cheating on what I had with Devin, but over time, Damon became my friend first, and I knew he wanted me to be happy—no matter what our relationship ended up being. Even DJ loved him as a second father; they'd go out and play football together and build things in the backyard. After having Tessa around, she became like a daughter to me. Seeing the brother-and-sister relationship she had with DJ grow into a special bond made it easy for me to love again.

I'd gone to the mall earlier and purchased a white-lace gown that had small beads stitched around the waist and back which helped cover my little baby-bump.

"I do," Damon said as his lips pulled into a smile.

"Do you, Jordan, take Damon to be your lawfully-wedded husband?" the minister asked.

I looked over Damon's shoulder at DJ, smiling and standing next to him as his best man. He nodded in agreement, and that warm feeling of home overwhelmed me.

"I do," I answered, tightening my hold on Damon's hand.

"With no just cause to deny, I now pronounce you husband and wife," the minister said. "You may kiss your bride." He closed the Bible and stepped back to give us room.

Damon moved in closer and lifted the veil from my face. He gently cupped my chin with one hand as I wrapped my arms around his waist, closing the space between us. He gazed down into my eyes. Our lips pressed together. His arms tightened around me, slowly moving down to grip my ass—he'd forgotten we were in front of the kids and a minister. I heard a low grumble, causing me to pull back, embarrassed at the display Damon and I were putting on in front of the kids and the minister. Damon apologized and shook hands with the minister as I bent and hugged DJ and Tessa.

"Yay! We're a family now!" DJ shouted joyfully and slapped hands with Damon.

"Yep, and you have a new little brother or sister coming soon," I told him as we walked out of the wedding hall and back to our hotel room to change for dinner.

We knew the kids would be excited, so we planned to get them full and loaded with snacks, before we celebrated—just the two of us.

The kids clapped and cheered once we arrived inside the secluded lounge that Damon had reserved earlier in the day. He shook hands with the owner, an old friend of his from college. Tessa climbed into the booth, and I slid in beside her. DJ came in next, and Damon sat on the outside, always in protective mode when we all went out together.

They had a special meal of steak, steamed vegetables, pasta, and chocolate cake prepared already. I couldn't drink because of the pregnancy, so the kids and I drank water as Damon held a glass of champagne. "I guess it's too late to back out now, Jordan," Damon joked, his fingers caressing my shoulders.

Before I could respond, his phone rang in his pocket, and he pulled it out. I saw his ex's name across the screen. I knew he'd told me they'd squashed the beef of her trying to take full custody of Tessa, but sometimes, females felt like if they couldn't have their man, then they'd take what he loved the most—and Bridget had tried her best. Damon wanted to cut her off, and I explained that Tessa needed her mom. She'd never forgive him if he cut all ties to her. If she played her role as Tessa's mom and didn't hurt her, we'd be fine. Before our trip to Vegas, I'd told him to let Tessa spend the night with her mom, so she wouldn't feel as though she was completely abandoned.

I watched as he ignored her call and turned his phone off. The kids laughed and talked as we had a stare down. Once the photo situation happened, I needed space, but Damon didn't agree. After our makeup session at his home, I spent two days away in our cabin, contemplating not spending the rest of my life with this man. It honestly felt like another death—until he'd shown up and argued, and we'd talked, made love, and did the same cycle all over again.

Taking a deep breath, I asked, "Does she know where you're at?"

The waitress placed our meals on the table. I helped DJ and Tessa cover themselves with napkins, so they wouldn't make a mess on the new clothes we'd bought them for the wedding.

Damon nodded and helped pass the plates around the table. "Bridget should be the last thing you're worried about, Choc. Enjoy this time away. The last thing we need is her drama interrupting our family," Damon explained, brushing a curl behind my ear and kissing my lips.

"Damon, we can't pretend she isn't a part of our family. At one point, you loved her, and she's the mother of your child," I said, sliding my hand into his.

Damon picked my hand up and placed a kiss on my wrist.

Not feeling up to ruining our happy occasion, I decided to leave the conversation alone until we arrived back home to have a sit down with Bridget. All her attempts to get Damon back had almost worked. At one point, I did allow her to get in the way of what we'd started to build, and Emery helped me see that giving her that much power wasn't healthy. If I let another woman tell me about my man and speak about what my relationship was, it would bring nothing but strife. Now that we were married, I wasn't there for the baby-momma drama.

A thin smile edged his lips. "Are we having fun yet?" he questioned, and the kids screamed and shouted in glee.

Mrs. Damon Adams. Damn, I need to hurry and get the kids to bed.

I glanced at his chiseled jawline and moist, thick lips as he leaned over to press a kiss to my lips.

"If you keep looking at me like that, I won't be able to hold off feeling the inside of that pussy," he said with a smile. "I'd rather not have the kids hear you screaming my name this early and traumatize them. I can't wait to get you in bed with your legs spread behind your head."

* * *

Two hours later, after the family dinner, we checked in with everyone back home, bathed the kids, and finally got them into bed. The presidential suite we stayed in had the kids on the lower level, and our bedroom upstairs. No interruptions, and nothing would be heard. After showering in the guest bathroom, I moisturized my skin with the coconut lotion Damon loved so much. Whenever I wore it, he couldn't keep his hands off me.

I stared at my little baby bump, barely showing, and wondered what our baby would be like. Would he or she have my nose or lips? Damon's complexion or eyes? A new journey was beginning for us, and the baby was the first surprise I'd had in a long time that made me feel fully okay with moving on and letting Damon into my heart. I finally understood that it didn't mean I was pushing Devin out; I was just making room in my heart for Damon and Tessa, along with the new baby.

I shook my head as I heard old-school Marvin Gaye music play. I guessed that was Damon's way of making sure the kids wouldn't hear him moaning loudly. I still remembered our first time, when he cursed me out, then explained afterwards that he'd never had mind-blowing sex so good that a woman had him moaning before.

I took the short, black-lace lingerie I'd brought with me and stepped into it without putting on panties or a

119

bra. He would have just ripped it off me anyway, so I'd rather not have dealt with having to buy more, since the owner at the local Victoria's Secret knew me by name. I also slid on my four-inch heels. Damon was pissed when we first found out about my pregnancy, and I still wore heels to work. Angela and Emery joked often about how he'd call them, demanding they stop feeding my shoe habit with trips to the mall. What could I say? This girl loved her Giuseppe heels. For tonight, I was wearing red, patent-leather pumps that popped against my skin tone. I touched up my blush and changed to my red Fenty Stunna lipstick. I looked myself over one more time and decided to keep my hair swept into a high bun.

I eased out of the bathroom and walked down to the kids' bedroom one more time to make sure they were good. I saw them knocked out in their beds with the covers pulled up.

I closed the door and walked upstairs, following a trail of roses that led to our bedroom. *Wonder when he had time to set this up?* I thought and replayed the last few hours we'd spent together. Damon had never left my side. He must have had the hotel decorate the suite. As I got closer, I heard John Legend's "All of Me," a reminder from Granny, who once told me that when I found the one, he would make me think about life in a different way. I'd find my peace, and no other could break that bond; all my highs, lows, and in-betweens would be fulfilled by the person standing next to me on life's road.

My mouth hung agape at the candles lighting a trail to Damon, standing with a single rose in his hand. He wore long, silk pajama pants. He was shirtless, showing off his broad shoulders, toned abs, and large hands, extended and ready to feel me up. I'd never seemed speechless around him before, but at that moment, I couldn't even remember my name. I was glad I was already pregnant. I knew Damon wouldn't let me out of bed for the rest of our time in Vegas.

"See something you like?" Damon asked, tilting his head and motioning for me to come inside.

"Mr. Adams," I questioned, "when did you have time to do all this without me catching on?"

"When you were out playing with the kids earlier. I made some calls and set things in motion."

As I walked into the room, Damon pulled me into his arms. I slid my hands around his neck, and his hands rubbed up and down my back, taking a hold of my ass and squeezing it as we kissed. I instinctively curled my lips around his tongue, and we explored each other like it was the first time—until someone rang the doorbell.

"Ignore them, Choc," he murmured. His sweet, warm breath lingered just above my swollen lips.

Whoever was ringing and banging on the door would end up waking the kids. I tried to get out of Damon's grip to see who it was, but he refused to give in.

"Baby, let me see who it is, so we can get rid of them," I whispered as he lifted my chin to deepen the kiss.

"Fuck them; they'll get the picture," Damon growled, walking me back to the bed.

"Damon! Damon!" We both pulled away at the loud shouting of a woman who sounded a lot like Bridget.

"Did you call—" I began.

"Jordan, don't even try to say some shit like that. You know damn well I wouldn't have called her up here. Let me get rid of her, so we can continue my plans." Damon picked his t-shirt up off the couch and slid into his slippers.

I didn't want him causing any bigger issues with her, so I jumped up to put my robe and shoes on, then followed him.

"What are you doing?" he asked.

"Following you," I responded.

"No, you're not. Stay here and get naked. This won't take long."

I waved off his comment as he turned to walk out and followed him. First, I checked on the kids to make sure the noise hadn't woken them. The bedrooms were right downstairs, near the front door.

Damon opened the door, and I stood to his right as Bridget's hand was in midair, about to knock again. We were both taken by surprise at her being here. It was Damon's turn to have Tessa. I knew she was on some bullshit, and I wasn't about to let her ruin our family trip.

Damon's mouth tightened in a grimace, and disgust twisted Bridget's mouth into a sneer. She glared at me as I stood there in a robe with the music still lightly playing.

"Why are you here, Bridget?" Damon growled.

"I need to speak with you privately," Bridget replied through clenched teeth.

"Is it life or death?" Damon asked.

Bridget jerked back in shock. "Can you put some clothes on or something?" Bridget taunted me sarcastically. "I need to talk to our man." She tried to walk inside.

"Whatever you have to say, you can say in front of us both," Damon said and wrapped an arm around my shoulder.

"I'm pregnant!" Bridget yelled.

I knew about her pregnancy already and clapped my

hands in front of her, letting her know she couldn't win this time. Damon informed me after she came to his office, trying to get under his skin and break us up.

"Congrats, anything else? I hate to rain on your parade, but Jordan already knows," Damon said.

Chapter Twenty-Five

Damon

The thought that Jordan would leave me over Bridget's false claim that she was pregnant by me was laughable. Did I sleep with her a few months back? Yes. Did I use protection? Hell yes! I knew the type of person Bridget was and getting involved with her the first time was a wake-up call for me. On top of that, I was madly in love with Jordan and was already planning on making her my wife back then.

Bridget stepped inside, and I closed the door, leaning my back against it as she took a seat on the couch. I was so angry I wanted to run upstairs and lock Jordan in our bedroom to keep her from leaving. At the same time, I needed to get Bridget to tell the truth and leave, so this wouldn't turn into a bigger issue.

"Bridget, I'm done," I said. "If the baby is mine—which I highly doubt because I used protection—then we will discuss joint custody when the time comes. Until then, you have to leave me alone," I explained with my hands in my pockets to keep from choking her to death. Every second, I had to think of Tessa and remind myself that she would grow up hating me if I put my hands on her mom.

"You're picking her over me and Tessa?" Bridget questioned curiously. She gestured upstairs and then pointed at herself.

"You mean my wife? Then, yes," I answered and walked away.

Bridget lifted her hand and gripped my elbow to stop me from leaving. "Please, tell me you didn't marry her, Damon. We both know that, deep down, it's always been you and me, from our first day in Mr. Theodore's biology class," Bridget stated somberly. I saw out of the corner of my eye that Jordan headed upstairs, shaking her head. A few minutes later, Jordan came downstairs. She was still in her robe, without her luggage. I was sure she'd have been dressed and halfway across the country by now.

"Babe—" I began.

"Shut up, Damon," Jordan interrupted me. "I'll deal with you in a minute. Bridget, listen up because I'm only going to say this once. Going forward, you will be dealing with our lawyer."

I parted my lips to respond, and Jordan stared at me, daring me to challenge her.

"Excuse me?" Bridget frowned and pushed out a heavy breath.

"We are too grown for this back-and-forth baby-momma drama. I let you get away with a lot because I was still torn between my feelings for Damon and my deceased husband. Now, we're married, and I'm officially Mrs. Adams. The games and you popping up and causing problems will not be tolerated any longer. If you have anything to say concerning Tessa or this new child which you claim Damon is the father, then you will go through our lawyer." She lifted an eyebrow.

Bridget's eyes widened. She looked between Jordan and me, thinking I would come to her defense.

"Don't look at my husband," Jordan snapped. "He's no longer your concern, sweetie. You're dealing with me now, and I'll handle all of Tessa's drop offs through our lawyer. Now, if you'll please leave, I'm ready to get back to my honeymoon—or I can call security."

I felt relieved at her boldness as she finally confronted Bridget and put her in her place. This new attitude was sexy and turning me on.

"I guess you'll be hearing from my lawyer, then," Bridget sassed, then turned her nose up at Jordan and walked out.

Jordan released a harsh breath and turned to walk away.

I stepped in front of her, closing the distance, determined not to let our first night as husband and wife get sidetracked with lies. "Choc, it's not true. You have to believe me. I did sleep with her, but it was when you and I had a break, and you told me to date other people."

"Why her, of all people, Damon?" Jordan asked, confused, laying her head on my chest.

"Familiarity, no other reason. She knew what I had with you, and that we'd just broken up for the second time, and I wasn't thinking clearly. I *did* use protection."

"I know. It just hurts that we'll have this dangling over our heads until the baby is born. Are you sure she's Tessa's mom?" Jordan inquired jokingly.

I engulfed her in my arms, kissing the top of her head, her cheeks, and her lips.

DJ and Tessa came out of their room, rubbing their

eyes in confusion. "Mommy, what's all that noise? I couldn't sleep," DJ said, patting her leg. We separated, and he squeezed between us, so she could pick him up. Tessa walked over to sit on the couch and turn the TV on.

"Shouldn't you two be in bed right now?" I chided, then turned the TV back off. My honeymoon night wouldn't be disturbed by anyone.

"We couldn't sleep with all that noise you and Mommy made," Tessa answered, puffing out her cheeks and pouting.

I bent to kiss her forehead, then picked her up to take her back to the room. "Sorry about that, chipmunk. We will be quieter going forward—or, at least, I will."

Jordan smacked me in the back of the head for my statement. I shrugged and leaned down to kiss her lips.

"Ohhh, that's gross, Daddy! No kissing." Tessa moved my head away from Jordan's, and we both laughed at her and DJ's facial expressions.

"Tessa, don't listen to your dad," Jordan said. "We apologize for waking you both up." She laid DJ down in his bed as I placed Tessa in the top bunk bed.

"Is Mommy okay, Daddy?" Tessa asked.

I didn't have the heart to tell her I didn't care whether she was okay or not, seeing as how she'd made it her life's mission to destroy any happiness I might have. However, when I looked into the eyes of my little princess, I vowed that I wouldn't let anything destroy her loving thoughts of her mom, so I answered with a half-truth to keep things in her world just as comfortable as they could be. "Your mom's fine, Tessa. She needed some help with something, and I didn't get it done in time, so she was upset. Don't you worry about your mom and me. We both love you, and Jordan loves you, as well.

How do you feel about our new family with Jordan and DJ?"

Tessa smiled at me with her eyes lit up in glee. "I get to be a big sister to Mommy's new baby."

The nervousness and tightness in my chest eased as I realized that she loved Jordan and DJ just as much as I did. I knew that if she didn't approve of our relationship, I would have had to give up my happiness. Even though she had her mother, deep down, Bridget wasn't the most present parent in her life. Often, I picked up the slack and showed up at parents' night at her school. Tessa could always count on her dad.

"How about tomorrow, we go out and hit up some stores? We can go shopping, then do a few rollercoaster rides."

Tessa leaned over and hugged me. I kissed her once again on the forehead and leaned down to do the same to DJ. Jordan walked away, heading toward our bedroom upstairs.

Overwhelmed by the events of tonight, I composed myself and focused on pleasing my wife and salvaging what was left of our wedding night. I entered our bedroom holding hands with my wife. We both blew all the candles out, and the music was turned off, but I wouldn't look back on this night years down the road with regrets.

I moved closer to the bed and pulled my shirt off, then pushed my pants down, leaving me in only my boxers. I lifted the covers and squeezed in closer to Jordan, then peeled one strap from her lingerie off her left shoulder. I trailed a kiss up her shoulder to her neck and behind her ear.

She moaned under her breath, and I felt goosebumps

as she squirmed in my arms. "Damon, go to sleep, baby." Jordan sighed and turned around to face me.

I shook my head in defiance and gently pushed her onto her back, pressing kisses down her chest and stopping at her breasts. I pinched and tugged on her nipple gently, then bit and licked her right breast and squeezed her left one. Jordan's soft lips parted in surrender, and she reached out to grip my face and pull me back up for a kiss.

"What about the noise?" Jordan questioned teasingly between kisses and giggled.

"Shut up," I demanded and ripped her lingerie down the middle.

She gasped and tried to cover her body.

"Don't you dare," I begged.

"Damon, I paid a lot for that outfit," she said. "You owe me $132." She narrowed her eyes in anger.

I lowered my head to kiss her on the lips again to shut her up.

Her cute pout slowly faded away as my head lowered to my favorite place: Her sweet sex. The prolonged anticipation was almost unbearable. I looked her over seductively one more time, then eased her lips open with my thumb and right index finger. I blew a cool breeze over her sex and felt her shiver weakly in my arms. My left arm wrapped around her legs to hold her steady. Again, I blew a cool breeze and followed up with my tongue, licking a straight line from her asshole to her lips.

"You still feel like we should stop?" I asked.

Her back arched off the bed, and she shook her head. Her juices were so sweet, I could feed off her every day for the rest of my life.

"Open your eyes, Choc, and watch me please you, baby," I said.

She was speechless in my arms. Normally, her moans radiated throughout the room. I guessed with all the commotion from earlier, she didn't want to wake the kids again.

I dove back in with my tongue, brushing against her swollen nub and switching between French kissing and biting.

"Damon..." Jordan called out in a whisper.

The touch of her hand was suddenly almost unbearable in its tenderness. The low whisper of her moan made me want her to never think of another man again. I felt a raw act of possession in knowing she was mine forever, and I savored the feeling of satisfaction once her juices spilled out onto the sheets.

"Yes, Mrs. Adams," I teased as her legs trembled, and she reached out to grip my head and push me away.

"Ahhh... wait... fuck!" Jordan screamed into the pillow. She twitched and shivered in my arms, coming down from her orgasm.

I couldn't wait to slide inside her as her husband. Not giving her time to recover, I slid my boxers down and centered my cock at her opening, then eased into her tight sex. I felt like a virgin all over again and stilled, not wanting to come too early and have her joke about our first night as husband and wife. My hand slid across her flat stomach, thinking about her having my baby. I ran a hand up her torso to her chin, then traced a fingertip across her lips, distracting her as I eased deeper into her sex.

"Shit!" I groaned, nuzzling my face against her neck.

"Mr. Adams, I love you," Jordan stated, as she kissed my chin. She curled against the curve of my body as I thrust into her faster. Her hips and back arched off the bed, meeting me thrust for thrust.

"Mmm... baby, you feel so good," I moaned into her ear and kissed her as I picked up her leg to raise it around my waist.

Our bed shook against the wall, and I knew that we would hear it from the kids tomorrow, but honestly, I didn't care. If I needed to buy out the entire toy store tomorrow to make up for the noise, then so be it, because I wouldn't be able to just have her for one round tonight.

"You, too... oh, God, Damon... please!" Jordan shouted as we both came together.

I fell on top of her, unable to move. We both tried to steady our breathing.

"Jordan, I love you," I said.

"I know," Jordan said, then curled into my arms.

Chapter Twenty-Six

Jordan

I tossed and turned in bed, feeling a pair of hands slowly moving downward, skimming either side of my thighs. "Baby, aren't you tired?" I suggested as Damon was between my legs once again. The pleasure was pure and explosive to my core.

"I could never get enough of you," Damon mumbled under his breath.

"I can tell from your morning wake-up call, Mr. Adams," I chortled and shot him a wide grin.

Today was our last day in Vegas, and I wanted to get the kids up before they ran in here and saw us half-naked again. Bad enough I was embarrassed about making so much noise during the night.

Damon chuckled and hovered over me with his hands on either side of my face. "It feels good to fall asleep next to you, Mrs. Adams," Damon stated with a grateful smile. He lowered his head, inching closer with his lips ready to invade my mouth for a kiss, not caring about morning breath. The warmth of his soft flesh was intoxicating. His hardness was ready to conquer my walls and give us both the pleasure we sought.

I did my best to keep the events of last night from messing up our time together, but we needed to discuss the Bridget situation before things got out of hand. "Baby, I hate to spoil the mood, but we need to talk with your lawyer about Bridget."

Concern grew on his face at the mention of Bridget's name. Damon was a patient man, but Bridget made a deep frown crease his brow. "Bridget and I don't have a situation. She can claim all she wants, but I refuse to give in to her games. We're here on our honeymoon with our kids. And I'm ready to spoil you and our new baby." Damon pulled away, with his legs drawn over the bed as he sat up. He looked away and delicately pinched the bridge of his nose as he closed his eyes.

I said nothing, just stared at him blankly while chewing the inside of my mouth. He was right in the sense that I was letting her win by coming between our time together as a family. She was in the past, and I was fully confident that he'd never cheat on me and break my heart. After listening to Emery and Granny, I realized I had to woman up and claim what was mine. I shifted behind him and wrapped my arms around his shoulders. I gently pressed a kiss behind his ear, his sensitive spot that turned him on. "I'm sorry, you're right," I said. "We should enjoy today and deal with her when we get back home to New York."

Damon swung around and tugged me close to his chest.

"I can't believe we're going to have three kids in a house under the age of seven," I said and brushed a kiss across his lips.

He reached around and gripped my waist, rubbing the arc of my hips and causing goosebumps to rise on my skin. "You know, I want more kids with you after this one. Even if it comes back that Bridget's carrying my baby, that doesn't stop us from trying for more babies, too, Choc. Don't let her win, baby." His expression was panicked, and he tightened his hold around my waist.

"I won't let her win, because what we have is unbreakable," I said. "We're having a little prince or princess, Mr. Adams." I pressed his right hand against my stomach.

His eyes bore into mine as he placed a kiss on my forehead. "You look beautiful pregnant," Damon replied. His sharp gaze landed on my stomach.

"Yeah," I replied. "All those late nights of you calling me and begging paid off."

He gently kissed my lips and smiled.

Suddenly, the kids burst into the room. "Daddy, what's going on?" Tessa questioned with her hair all over her head and her socks halfway on. She was a rough sleeper like me and never woke up the same way she went to bed.

DJ followed her with a bowl of cereal in his hand and milk stains all over his clothes. Damon had the suite already fitted with groceries for the kids prior, so we didn't have to depend on room service, unless it was necessary.

"Tessa, DJ, we have something to talk to you about," Damon said. "DJ, why didn't you wait for us to prepare breakfast?"

He placed me down on my feet, so we could both gather our robes to cover up. During the night, after round three in bed, we'd showered and put some clothes on, just in case the rugrats came into our room before we woke up.

"I was hungry," DJ answered, shrugged, and turned the TV on in our room.

I took the remote out of his hands and turned the volume down, so we could have a family meeting. "DJ, you know with the new baby coming soon, things are going to be busier in our house," I told him, making eye contact with him to make sure he understood. For so long, it had been just him and me. Then Damon came into the picture, and I had to juggle my time between them both. On top of work, it became a balancing act. Having Tessa every other day and wanting her to feel welcome could have caused another issue, but DJ was happy and never let on if he had a problem with my relationship.

He nodded and continued eating Captain Crunch, spilling a little of the milk on the bed. Tessa climbed into her father's lap, and I sat beside DJ, rubbing his head. Damon entwined our fingers in comfort, and I smiled back in relief.

"This means Mommy will have to do a better job of balancing her time, but I want you to know you are always my priority."

"How are babies made?" Tessa asked. My heart beating so fast, I thought it would pop out of my chest.

DJ and Tessa both smiled in glee. "When do we pick him up?" DJ asked.

I shifted my weight from one foot to the other. The conversation of babies had never come up, and his eyes popped, and warmth spread across his face. Laughing at his expression, Damon kissed Tessa on the cheek and placed her on the bed. He brushed his hand across DJ's head in comfort, giving him a kiss on the forehead. Deep down, I felt like Devin sent Damon into my life because he knew I wouldn't be able to move on without his love. Everything that Damon was reminded me of Devin, and at the same time, they were different people. Devin was always joking; he was the life of the party and so spontaneous. Damon was very laidback and quiet, wearing his heart on his sleeve—but don't get it confused. They were both alpha males, possessive if anyone hurt someone they loved.

He reached over and stood behind me, nuzzling his nose against my neck. "DJ, the baby won't be here for a little while. In the meantime, we have plans to take you guys around Vegas and hit up some rollercoasters. Does that sound like fun?"

The kids clapped and jumped on the bed in joy.

Damon whispered in my ear, "You're welcome."

I turned my head to the side and mouthed, *"Thank you,"* in return. Having to explain the ways of childbirth wasn't on the agenda while we were in Vegas.

* * *

Six hours later, we'd finished up at the mall and let the kids ride all the rides. I was even able to get us in to see the latest animated movie, *Boss Baby*. All day was spent pleasing the kids and letting them enjoy themselves, before we would head back home tomorrow. Damon needed to get back to work, and my vacation hours were almost up. Already, I was getting calls and messages from Emery and Angela about the wedding and how things went. I was saving the news about Bridget for when I spoke to them in person. I knew that between Angela and Granny, jail was an option.

I wasn't Granny's grandchild biologically, but she cared about me just as much as she cared about Emery and Angela. Plus, I needed to let Devin's parents know about all the changes happening in our lives. I would never let Devin's memory die; he was the love of my life, my first everything, and DJ's father, but I saw this as another chance for me to love and be loved.

As we walked into the suite, my phone vibrated in my hand. Damon took my bags out of my hands and helped the kids pack up their things. This was our last night, so we'd just have dinner in the room and head to bed early for our flight. One good thing about having a rich husband was the luxury of nice things. Damon flying us out on a private jet was a nice amenity I couldn't give up.

Emery: How was the wedding?

Me: It was nice, and you know, I was emotional and cried.

Angela: Forget the wedding. How was the honeymoon?

Emery: Is that all you can think about?

Me: Probably, since she turned up pregnant.

Angela: Oh, you really can't talk.

I'm not the only one pregnant, and besides, this was an oops baby.

Emery: What the hell is an oops baby, Angela?

Me: Yes, please tell us.

Angela: Oops, I fell on some good dick and couldn't get off ;)

Emer: LOL, you're a mess. Did you tell Brent yet?

Angela: This is about Jordan's wedding.

Leave my business out of this, ma'am.

Me: Angela, you really should talk with him. What are you going to do?

Wait until the kid turns 18, then let Brent know he's the potential daddy?

I walked into the kitchen to grab a bottle of water as Damon came out of the living room with the kids following him. "Room service will be here soon, baby," Damon said. "I ordered you soup and salad." He leaned down to kiss me on the lips.

"What did you order for yourself and the kids?" I asked nosily.

"Burger and fries for the kids. I ordered a steak, potatoes, garlic bread, and green beans, and cheesecake for dessert."

"What makes you think I didn't want that?" I chided, then went back to my group text message.

Angela: Can we focus on one pregnant lady at a time?

Brent's not thinking about me, and it's probably not his baby.

Emery: Are you saying you're seriously going to hide this from him, Angela? Before anything, Brent's our friend. Yes, you guys had a sexual relationship, but you can't handle this situation in silence and hide.

I saw the beginnings of a message from Angela pop up and then disappear. She probably felt we'd been too hard on her. Angela could be selfish at times, and after a while, Brent had finally had enough and wouldn't let her run the relationship by only giving him half of herself.

Damon grabbed the phone out of my hand before I could reply and turned it off. "This is our last night as a family. Emery and Angela can wait for you to get back to deal with their issues. Tonight, it's about us celebrating our new addition to the family."

"You're just trying to—" I started to respond, but the doorbell rang.

Damon kissed me on the lips and ran to open the door as Tessa followed him. The smell of the food caused my stomach to growl. I'd had lunch while we were out, but the baby was making me hungry all over again. I picked up my phone again to reply to the girls.

Me: Ladies, my husband demanded I spend some time with him.

We fly out tomorrow morning, so let's do lunch
and catch up after I drop the kids off.

Emery: Sybil's?

Angela: Sybil's. I could use her famous margaritas right about now.

Me: Okay, first off, crazy girl, you're pregnant, and second, let's meet at noon.

Angela: I thought you could have alcohol and coffee while pregnant?

Me: Oh, Lord, this is going to be a long nine months with you.

You can only have wine, and that's in moderation.

Angela: Who the hell made up that rule?

Me: God.

Angela: Well, didn't Joseph and Mary have a few sips
of the stronger stuff once every blue moon?

Emery: Angela, go to bed, and tomorrow, we're taking you to church.

Angela: Too late for church, honey. I've done every sin in the Bible.

Me: Granny gonna get you.

Angela: Who you think I learned everything from?

Me: Good night.

I shut my phone off and focused on my family for the rest of the night.

* * *

Two weeks later, we moved in together. My pregnancy was full-on now, and I was showing. The doctor said I was on my feet too much, and all the excitement of the wedding, Bridget, and work had caused me to stress a little.

I still hadn't told the girls about Bridget. We'd stuck to our word and contacted Damon's lawyer. She wasn't a huge problem anymore, as far as Tessa and co-parenting. The doctor told us we could get a blood test done before the baby was born to find out if Damon was the father, and she agreed without an issue. She was still representing a few of his clients, and a part of me wanted to tell him to end his contract with her, but as a woman with a child, I understood that she needed to work. Bridget hadn't caused any problems since the blowup in Vegas; she'd stayed in her own lane and hadn't bashed Damon to the media.

However, our pregnancy and wedding was all over the news. All the gossip blogs talked about Damon Adams marrying a local schoolteacher with a kid. They made it seem as though I were someone he'd just picked up off the street.

Today, I'd left Damon in bed. The kids stayed home with him, and I'd agreed to go to Granny's house for lunch.

I pulled up right as Angela was getting out of her car. She looked to be arguing on the phone, as her hands flew all over the place. I got out of my car and met her at hers. "Whatever," she declared and hung up the phone.

"Who was that?" I asked, following her into the house.

She waved me off. Inside, we heard loud yelling and screaming from the front room. The smell of food wafted through the house. JJ was on the floor, playing with his toys, as Jackson and Pops sat watching the NFL draft.

"Hey, guys," Angela said. She walked over to JJ and bent to kiss him on the cheek, then did the same to Pops, who was sitting in the same chair he had for the last thirty years.

Jackson stood and hugged us both, then took his plate off the table and walked off toward the kitchen.

"Pops, how are you doing?" I inquired.

"The old man is doing good, Jordan," he answered. "Surrounded by my grandkids and loving on my wife; don't get no better than that." He extended his hand to rub my belly.

"Please, keep the mention of having sex with your wife to a minimum," Angela said. "That's gross, Pops." She snorted and wagged her finger at him.

He cast only the slightest of glances at her before focusing back on the TV.

Angela pouted and stomped off toward the kitchen. I followed her.

"What's with all that stomping and carrying on?"

Granny questioned as she stood at the stove, taking the cornbread out of the oven.

Jackson was hovering over Emery, making googly eyes at her and rubbing her pregnant belly. Angela looked down at her phone as it rang in her hand and scoffed at whoever was calling.

"Angela was messing with Pops," I snitched, and Angela rolled her eyes at me.

"You roll your eyes again, and I'll snatch them out your head, little girl," Granny spat out at Angela. Her back had been facing us all, but somehow, she always knew what was going on.

"I wasn't rolling my eyes," Angela muttered under her breath.

"Jackson, leave us alone, so I can have some time with my girls," Granny demanded. "Emery isn't going anywhere." She passed him a plate of spaghetti, cornbread, black-eyed peas, and greens. In all the time I'd known Granny, she'd never just made a simple meal. No matter the time or the day, if she was cooking, we could expect a full meal.

Jackson went back for seconds for him and Pops and took both plates to the living room and left us alone. Angela sat next to Emery, and I sat across from them as Granny placed food in front of all of us.

Then, she sat at the head of the kitchen table, and we waited for her to start the conversation. "Is the Bridget situation handled, or do I need to get my gun?" she asked.

"How do you know about Bridget?" I picked up my fork and ate the greens and cornbread, remembering to take some food to go for the family, since she'd made enough for an entire army.

"Granny, you can't go around shooting people,"

Emery said. "We talked about this, remember? With Anthony?"

Granny gave a dismissive wave of her hand. "Fuck that boy—excuse me, Lord," Granny said and held her palms toward the sky.

"How can you curse and then ask the Lord for forgiveness?" Angela asked with an arched brow. "I don't think it works like that."

"The Lord works in many ways, Angela," Granny said. "The same as your lust guided you to keep your legs open to many men and come up pregnant. He didn't seek to cast you out. Now, the women at the church might look at you different, but the Lord and Granny will always love you."

Angela's mouth fell open. Emery dropped her fork in shock and covered her mouth to hide the lopsided grin that lit up her face.

"Don't you worry about how I know about the Bridget situation," Granny continued. "I have contacts in high places. Besides, I talked with your parents at church, and they told me about her messing with Damon for custody of Tessa."

"Damon's lawyer worked up an agreement," I replied. "After she burst in on us in Vegas, we planned to have a co-parenting setup through a lawyer and Damon's parents. She hasn't bothered us since."

"Well, don't forget to let me know when you get the results of the blood test. Everybody at church is talking," Granny explained.

Angela stood to get more food, right as her phone rang on the table. I looked over and saw the name "Robert" flash across the screen. I hoped she hadn't brought another guy into the situation; she was already dealing with two men and a baby on the way.

"We scheduled it," I replied. "It's just wait and see now. No matter the outcome, I will support Damon, and if it's his child, I'll help him raise it. It's partially my fault, since I broke up with him during the time, and he fell into her trap."

Angela sat back down and replied to the call with a text message. A snarl ran across her face.

"Trouble in paradise?" I asked.

Angela's expression sobered. "What are you talking about?" She shoved more food into her mouth as a look passed between her and Granny.

"This Robert guy, or whoever you're dating now," I responded. "Your phone hasn't stopped ringing since we got here."

She glanced down at her phone, right as another text message came through.

"Is it someone we know?" Emery questioned.

Jackson walked into the kitchen with JJ right behind him.

"Robert's a friend, nothing more," Angela said. "We should be focusing on your party coming up and celebrating the new baby." She tucked a lock of hair behind her ear.

"Sweetness, you know Robert from the office," Jackson said, giving us all of Angela's business. "He works in the marketing department. Remember? He was the one who oversaw the last campaign for the club."

Angela rolled her eyes at the ceiling.

"Oh... I remember him," Emery answered. "He's cute, Angela."

Jackson's eyebrows rose in shock. "Sweetness, don't

ever say another man is cute around me, or we will have a problem." He kissed her on the cheek and walked off.

JJ headed toward Granny and reached up for her to pick him up.

"I guess he told you," Granny said.

Emery waved her off, and we all continued eating and joking for the next two hours, catching up and making plans for my upcoming party.

Chapter Twenty-Seven

Angela

Granny had called me over to help celebrate Jordan's engagement, wedding, and pregnancy announcement. At first, I'd declined because I always avoided being around Brent, but whenever Granny called and cursed me out, then I had to do what she wanted.

My makeup was a little light today, just a little mascara and lip-gloss. I checked out my long, flowy maxi-dress with the side pockets and off-the-shoulder sleeves that hopefully covered any signs of me being pregnant.

As soon as Emery and Jordan found out, they'd pushed me to tell Brent, but I was still nervous about whether he'd be open to the possibility of being a father, now that we'd broken up.

During my years of dating, my goal had always been to not fall in love. After dealing with abandonment issues, I didn't want to put my all into another situation just to be disappointed. Somehow, Brent had torn my walls down and helped me love. Brent thought I kept him at arm's length, but deep inside, I was in love with him.

There was a knock on my car window. "Are you coming inside?" Granny asked, standing at my car door with her hands on her hips.

I grabbed my purse and the present I'd purchased for Jordan and Damon, then unlocked the door. "Old lady, why are you out here?" I sassed. "Did you think I wouldn't show up?" I put my hand on my hip, imitating her posture.

"Girl, your best bet is to get inside, so everybody can start eating before this food gets cold. I have a date tonight, and you're blocking my time."

"Date with who?" I questioned.

"Pops! My husband, of course. Now, what did you bring me?" Granny inquired, peering into my bags.

I followed her into the house and heard loud laughing and talking in the kitchen. I noticed Emery and her parents in the kitchen with JJ. "Hello, family," I greeted them. "What's going on?"

"She finally came out of her cave!" Emery cried. "Granny, did you have to bribe her to get her here?"

"Emery, hush," Granny chastised. "You're the last person who should talk about someone staying away. Let's not talk about your secrets, honey." She picked JJ up off the floor and kissed his forehead.

"Granny, you always take Angela's side," Emery said and rolled her eyes.

"Whatever, Emery," I said. "I'm not staying long, anyway. I have a few appointments, so I have to get back to the salon."

"You might as well get comfortable," Pops joked. "You're staying to eat and hang out." He hugged me as I neared him to head outside to the patio.

"How are you feeling, Pops?" I asked. "Granny told

me you've been doing good, eating better, and taking her out on the town, keeping her young."

"You know, *she* keeps *me* young," he replied. "How are you feeling? I didn't say anything to you about this little bundle of joy you're carrying, but I'm excited for another grandbaby."

Granny passed me a glass of lemonade as I took my phone out of my purse and moved my appointments around for another day. I could tell this would be a lengthy family celebration. "Thanks, Granny," I said. "I'm coming to terms with things, Pops. Who all is here, anyway?" I inquired.

"Jordan's family, Damon's parents, and the usual people," Emery responded. "Brent and a few friends from church."

We all took our drinks and followed Emery's parents to the backyard celebration. Emery had hired the same decorator from Jackson's party last year when he'd signed a new team. They had gold-and-silver balloons hanging around, white linen tablecloths, and a kids' section with games, toys, and a small candy stand.

"Wow, Anthony was invited?" I asked.

"Girl, we've moved on so far from his drama with Teresa," Emery responded. "I told Jordan when we started planning this that I'm fine with him coming around. I've forgiven him, and Jackson has no problems with him—as long as he doesn't get out of line."

"I guess," I replied, "but if that happened to me, I would've cut his dick off and made him sleep with one eye open."

"Your mind is so warped," Emery answered.

I shrugged and picked up a plate to fill it with barbeque, mac and cheese, and Granny's famous potato salad. "Hey, Damon," I greeted him. "Congrats on every-thing." I gave him a one-armed hug as I filled my plate. Jordan walked up behind him and kissed his lips.

"Thanks, Angela," Damon replied. "I appreciate you coming today and celebrating with us. It was a long road to get your girl to see I was for real, and now, we're married and about to have a baby." He hugged Jordan close and rubbed his hand over her pregnant stomach.

I felt the love in the air and looked across the yard at all the couples: Emery's parents; Jordan's parents—hell, even Anthony had someone who'd helped settle him down. I didn't see Brent around. I guess he'd decided to not come.

"He couldn't come because of work," Jordan said, noticing me looking around. "He was closing a big deal today."

Releasing a breath, I turned back around and picked up another glass of lemonade, then sat at the table with Granny, Emery, and Pops. The deejay played music, and some of the kids got up and danced. Damon pulled Jordan into his lap and watched as Tessa tried to follow JJ's steps and floss. We all laughed and cheered her on as I danced in my seat.

"All right, now, little girl," Granny scolded me. "Don't get too hot with that little ass popping in your seat."

Everyone laughed at her, putting me on the spot.

"Granny, I learned my moves from you," I said. "Stop hating. Besides, didn't you get Pops because of your dance moves?" I moved more in my seat as the music played.

Her eyes narrowed in anger, and she flicked me off. Emery snickered next to her. DJ ran over to the table, right as Brent walked toward us. I smelled his cologne as he came near.

"Auntie Angela and Uncle Bee, when is your baby due?" DJ asked, and the entire table went quiet.

Brent laughed at DJ's question and playfully tickled him. "Little man, Angela isn't pregnant," Brent said.

Frozen in place, I looked at Emery and Granny, praying they could help get me out of this situation. Everyone stared back at me, not making any eye contact with Brent.

"Yes, she is, Uncle Bee," DJ said. "I'm going to be a big cousin, right, Mommy?"

Jordan fumbled with her hands, nervous about him blowing my cover. She picked DJ up to take him away from the table.

"The only person who's pregnant next to Emery is Jordan," Brent insisted. "No way a man would get Angela pregnant."

"Excuse me?!" I exploded.

"Angela, come on now," Brent said. "We both know you're not mother material. You've never had the time or focus to be someone's mother."

I stood and rubbed my stomach. I was four months along. I was a thick girl, so you could hardly tell, with me already having a little pouch. I hadn't been with anyone since I found out. I was trying to come to terms with who the father was. I had planned on calling Jeremy next week and letting him know it was a possibility that he could be the father.

Brent stopped laughing, and his face went completely frozen. His eyebrows furrowed, and his hands tightened into fists. The anger across his face was something I didn't want to see because I knew he was hurt and disappointed. "When did you find out?" Brent asked. "Who's the father?"

The lump in my throat grew and caused me to stumble over my answer. Damon and Jackson stood and tried to pull Brent away. Granny continued eating as Pops shook his head.

"We can talk about this later," I replied. "Today is about Jordan and Damon."

Brent shook his head in frustration and walked off.

I decided to follow him to smooth things over. "Brent, please listen to me. I didn't want to tell you like this, okay?" I tried to grip his hand to stop him.

He jerked away from me and headed into the house, where he stopped and turned around, facing me with an angry scowl. "You have to be the most selfish bitch I've ever met!" Brent shouted.

"I understand you're upset, so I'll let your little comment slide, but don't let that word slip out of your mouth again."

Brent waved me off and moved closer to my face, seething. His lips were so beautiful and plump. I shook away my horny thoughts and focused on explaining the situation.

His gaze wandered slowly down my body. "Angela, you need to realize that I'm not running after you anymore. That's why I broke up with you in the first place. You're so selfish and only want things your way. You always forget about my needs."

A cold tremor ran through my body. "What do you want from me?"

"You piss me off!" Every fiber of his body shivered in anger.

"I'm sorry," I whispered.

Emery and Jordan came inside.

Brent looked behind me and shook his head in frustration. "How long did you know?" he questioned them both.

No one answered, and he turned to walk out. I reached out to stop him, but Emery and Jordan stopped me from going after him. I broke down crying in their arms. They gripped me close as Granny came trickling in with a plate of food.

"Calm down, Angela," Emery said. "You can't get stressed. It'll upset the baby." She rubbed my back as Jordan helped comfort me.

"He hates me!" I cried out.

Epilogue

Jordan

I was in the hospital with DJ and Tessa, who sat on the floor, playing, as my parents and Damon's parents waited for the birth of our baby girl. We'd decided on a name a few months back: Isabella Adams. After our Vegas elopement, moving in together, and making room in my heart for Damon, we became a big family. Devin's parents loved Damon and Tessa; she even spent the night sometimes when DJ would stay over. They basically adopted her as a second grandchild. I felt like this was a second chance at love, and I knew Devin was here, watching over us all.

"Choc, how you feeling, baby?" Damon said and bent to kiss my lips. He was wearing scrubs with his face mask around his neck and rubbing my stomach.

"So far, I'm fine," I replied. "She's just moving around a lot. I can tell she's going to take after DJ and drive us crazy."

"Honey, we'll take the kids down to the cafeteria to get something to eat and give you some privacy," Mom said.

The doctor walked in with the nurse, checked my vitals, and informed me that it was time. I couldn't wait to meet my baby girl. We'd recently decorated her room and upgraded Tessa and DJ's room, so they'd feel included with the new baby coming.

"Thanks, Mommy," I said. "Are Angela and Emery outside?"

"They are, along with everyone else," Mom replied. "Focus on yourself and this little girl. Angela will be fine."

My mom had tried to keep me out of the drama between Angela and Brent after our wedding celebration and baby shower. Brent hadn't talked to us or Angela for the past few months. It was hard because we'd been best friends since college, but he felt betrayed by us—even though he continued hanging with the guys. Emery and I should have told him about Angela. When she hit her second trimester, she decided to get a blood test and invited Brent, so they could find out if he was the father. Jeremy was still in the picture, and he knew Brent was the father. Angela had continued to date him and kept Brent updated with doctor's appointments. He'd come today and buried his anger to be there for the birth of our baby.

"Choc, what did I say about your friends?" Damon said.

"Stay out of their business and focus on my own... ugh! This little girl is ready to come out," I moaned, wrapping my hand around Damon's as the contraction came.

"Exactly. From this day forward, focus on our family, because soon, I'm knocking you up with another baby, Choc," Damon boasted as the doctor put my feet up in the stirrups, and the nurse checked my vitals.

"Damon, I love you, but there's no way I'm having any more kids."

"Okay, Choc, you say that now—until I do that little thing you like," Damon said.

With his hands rubbing up and down my arms, I felt a little flushed and warm inside, reminiscing about him pleasing me so well between my legs. "Don't threaten me. Besides, we can talk about another child in a few years. Let me get back to work first, and then we can see about more kids," I explained.

"All right, Mr. and Mrs. Adams," the doctor said. "Are you ready to meet your little Isabella?"

We both nodded, and the doctor told me to move down a little lower. He had Damon help keep my leg pushed up toward my chest. The pressure started, and he said to push.

* * *

Four hours later, Isabella was in Damon's arms. He hijacked her away from everyone.

Granny stood in front him with her hands on her hips and her lips puckered into a pout. "Give me my grandbaby, Damon," she said. "You've refused to pass her around for the last two hours."

"Granny, did you wash your hands?" Damon asked. "Newborns' lungs are fragile."

Granny flicked him on the forehead, and we all laughed at her. "Boy, how are you going to tell me anything about a newborn? This body has given life—and taken it if you mess with my family. So, I suggest you hand over my grandbaby, before you see these hands, little boy," she boasted.

Everyone in the room laughed.

"Jordan, I know you ain't laughing," Damon said.

"Nothing little about me, baby." He frowned, handing Isabella over.

"Baby, I'm sorry," I said. "You know Granny can get a little overzealous."

"Oh, his little feelings are hurt," Angela joked.

"You're the last person who should be commenting on someone's relationship," Brent said.

"Who invited you, anyway?" Angela muttered and sat back on the couch in the hospital room.

Brent's eyes held hers. I knew it would be a long road for them to get back to a positive place. Angela was secretly in love with him, and she wouldn't tell him, so Emery and I had to deal with her mood swings. Some days, she was in love, and some days, she hated him. Hopefully, having Isabella around would make them come together and be the best godparents they could be, because I needed my friend back.

I cleared my throat and decided to ask them while we were sitting in the room together. I knew Brent wanted to stay as far away from the group as possible. "So, Damon and I wanted to ask you guys a question. Since you both are here today, we wanted to see if you'd both be interested in being Isabella's godparents."

Angela and Brent stared at each other, then looked over at me and Damon. Angela smiled and headed over to hug me. Brent followed and slapped hands with Damon. Granny passed Isabella to Damon, then pushed Brent toward Angela.

"How much does that pay?" Angela asked.

"Angela, shut up!" everyone in the room yelled, and Isabella started crying. Granny nudged Brent to talk to Angela. It was getting late, and I wanted to feed Isabella and put her to sleep.

"Choc, your family and friends are crazy," Damon said. "What did I sign up for?" A teasing smile spread across his face.

"You signed up to heal my heart," I replied, "and I'll thank you every day for the rest of my life."

* * *

Follow a Second chance romance here "**Heart of Stone Book 3 Angela and Brent**" https://books2read.com/u/31rx9l

Get into a One night stand romance with **Jessica and Joseph**

Heart of Stone Book 3.5 https://payhip.com/b/HGP1

Heart of Stone Book 4 Jessica and Joseph https://books2read.com/u/4NXyPG

If you want more "Mafia Romance, why not try **"Antonio and Sabrina Book 2" Click here** https://books2read.com/u/bpED6g

Have you read *yet* **"Temptation?"** That is a stand-alone contemporary, sports, curvy girl romance. Check it out here https://books2read.com/u/mle1Vv

Are you interested in Mafia romance? Check into *Antonio & Sabrina: Struck in Love, Books* 1 https://books2read.com/u/4AxKLo

* * *

Check out **Aydin a grumpy boss, bodyguard romance** here https://books2read.com/u/mBwaOy .Follow my standalone opposites attract, age gap, military romance "**Exposed**" https://books2read.com/u/bQyYZe .

Are you a fan of sports romance? Then download one-night stand, billionaire romance "**Refuel**" https://books2read.com/u/boDyDA. Also, follow it up with workplace, sports romance "**Pressure**" https://books2read.com/u/3Ly1r7 .

If you love romantic comedy, fake relationships, enemies to lovers, find it here, "**Something Gained.**" Click the link https://books2read.com/u/baGLYy .

Any fan of forbidden romance, political? Check out "**Mutual Agreement**" https://books2read.com/u/mgzzWX a steamy romance. Pre-order the full novel of "**Nasir**" here click the link here.

Have you checked out "**She's All I Need**" click here https://books2read.com/u/49lkeW a sports, opposites attract romance. What about dark romance that has everything from steamy romance, opposites attract, suspense, thriller, celebrity, and more "**Joaquin Fuertes Book 1**" https://books2read.com/u/mvZlgV

Catch up with favorite characters in this holiday short romance which includes spoilers. https://books2read.com/u/bzd59G

Playlist

1. Janet Jackson, "So Deep"
2. Maxwell, "'til the Cops Come Knockin'"
3. Whitney Houston, "You Give Good Love"
4. Jill Scott, "He Loves Me"
5. Beyoncé, "Rocket"
6. Adele, "Someone Like You"
7. Mario: "Let Me Love You"
8. Carl Carlton, "She's a Bad Mamma Jamma"
9. Mariah Carey, "Breakdown"
10. Faith Hill, "Baby, You Belong"
11. Alicia Keys & Maxwell, "Fire We Make"
12. Kelly Clarkson, "Love So Soft"
13. Joe, "All the Things (Your Man Won't Do)"
14. Bob Marley & the Wailers "Waiting in Vain"
15. Aretha Franklin, "You Make Me Feel Like A Natural Woman"
16. Tamia, "Sandwich and Soda"

Reader Questions:

Email responses to <u>info@304publishing.com</u>

    1. Do you think Angela's really pregnant?

    2. Do you think Granny should cut Pop's a break?

    3. Should Emery and Jackson set boundaries for family and friends?

Heart of Stone series

Heart of Stone Book 1 Emery and Jackson
https://books2read.com/u/boWPAV
Heart of Stone Book 1.5
https://payhip.com/b/kWg7
Heart of Stone Book 2 Jordan and Damon
https://books2read.com/u/ba2OMx
Heart of Stone Book 3.5 Bottoms Up
https://payhip.com/b/HGP1
Heart of Stone Book 3 Angela and Brent
https://books2read.com/u/31rx9l
Heart of Stone Book 4 Jessica and Joseph
https://books2read.com/u/4NXyPG

Antonio and Sabrina Series

Order of Reading
The Early Years-A Prequel
https://books2read.com/u/49Zjnw
Ruthless Struck In Love Book 1
https://books2read.com/u/4AxKLo
Savage Struck In Love Book 2
https://books2read.com/u/bpED6g
Beast Struck In Love Book 3
https://books2read.com/u/3LpgdJ
Janice and Carlo Captivated By His Love
https://books2read.com/u/b6je6M
Brutal Struck In Love Book 4
https://books2read.com/u/4NQyE9
Stolen-Fuertes Mafia Cartel Book 1
https://books2read.com/u/mvZlgV
Saved-Fuertes Mafia Cartel Book 2
https://books2read.com/u/4DWwLd
Redemption Struck In Love Book 5
https://books2read.com/u/b5kZ8O

Betrayal- Fuertes Mafia Cartel Book 3
https://books2read.com/u/4A5LGp

Catalogue of Releases

The Early Years-A Prequel Short Story
Struck in Love 1, 2, 3,4,5
Heart of Stone, Book 1 (Emery & Jackson)
Heart Of Stone Book 1.5 Emery &Jackson A Valentine's Day Short
Janice and Carlo: Captivated By His Love
Heart of Stone, Book 2 (Jordan and Damon)
Temptation
Heart of Stone, Book 3 (Angela and Brent)
Bottoms Up Heart of Stone, Book 3.5(Jessica and Joseph Short
Cocky Catcher
Bossy Billionaire
Love Shorts:A Collection of Short Stories
Stolen Fuertes Mafia Cartel Book 1
Saved Fuertes Mafia Cartel Book 2
Exposed (Salvation Society Novel)
Betrayal Fuertes Mafia Cartel Book 3
Refuel(A Driven World Novel)
Pressure(A Driven World Novel)

Until Serena(HEA World Novel)
Exposed (Salvation Society Novel)
Heart of Stone, Book 4 (Jessica and Joseph)
She's All I Need
Something Gained(Romantic Comedy)
Thank you so much for reading, and if you enjoyed the crazy ride and decide to leave a review, we'd truly appreciate the support.

What's Next

Want to know what happens next?

Follow me on my website to catch the next release.

Reviews are the lifeblood of the publishing world. They're read, appreciated, and needed.

Please consider taking the time to leave a few words on your review platform of choice.

Sign up for updates and sneak peaks at the site below. www.chiquitadennie.com

304 Publishing Company

The home of authors African American, Interracial, Women's Fiction, Fantasy, Erotic, and Contemporary Romance novels. Along with Thriller, Suspense, Poetry, Beauty, and Style Books. Thank you for taking the time out to visit. Join our mailing list to stay updated with new releases and blog posts.

Acknowledgments

I want to dedicate this to my team that helps me behind the scenes, from my editors, test readers, graphic designers, and the list goes on. Truly appreciate each of you for keeping me on my toes.

About the Author

Chiquita Dennie is an author of Contemporary, Romantic Suspense, Erotic, Thriller, Mystery, and Women's Fiction. Chiquita lives in Los Angeles, CA. Before she started writing contemporary romance, she worked in the entertainment industry on notable TV shows such as The Dr Phil Show, The Tyra Banks Show, American Idol, and Deal or No Deal. But her favorite job is the one she's now doing full time: writing romance.

A best-selling author and award-winning filmmaker, her first short film Invisible was released in summer 2017 and screened in multiple festivals and won for Best Short Film. Also, she hosts a podcast that showcases the latest in beauty, business, and community called "Moscato and Tea." Her debut release of Antonio and Sabrina Struck In Love has opened a new avenue of writing that she loves.

If you want to know when the next book will come out, please visit her website at http://www.chiquitaden nie.com, where you can sign up to receive an email for her next release.